Yesterday's Tears

SAM CHEEVER

It might be a murder from decades ago, but it still has its claws in the present...and someone seems determined to drag Anna into it.

It's never a good idea to spend too much time in a haunted mansion, and Anna's favorite cowboy ghost does his best to talk her out of it. But the opportunity to pick from the beautiful antiques left to her in a Crocker resident's will is just too tempting for Anna and Pratt to pass up. So they're going in...

They're prepared to deal with a few cold spots. Maybe the occasional flickering light. But what Anna and the boys weren't counting on was bumping up against the ghost of Josiah Baumgartner, a contemporary of Joss' from the 1800s. And when Josiah claims the old woman who lived in the house hid his bones around the place, Anna agrees to help him find them. But something much darker is at work there. And, unfortunately for our happy little gang of antique hunters...Anna seems to have unwittingly stepped right into the middle of it.

GLOSSARY

Since Joss and Bess are from America's colorful past, I thought it might be good to provide a glossary of the colloquialisms they use in the text of this book. Some of them don't require explanation. I haven't included those, but the more interesting ones certainly could use a little clarification. Even within context, the meanings of some of the following terms can't be easily ascertained.

Absquatulated: to disappear

All-overish: uncomfortable

Backing and filling: waffling

B'hoy: rowdy boy, ruffian

Cap the climax: beat all

Catchin' a weasel asleep: referring to something that's unlikely

Chirk: cheerful

Codfish aristocracy: a contemptuous term for rich business people

Coot: a simpleton

Cotton to: take a liking to

Fix one's flint: to settle a matter

Fyst: A worthless dog, a mongrel

G'hal: rowdy girl, ruffian

Gotham City: New York City

Grab the little end of the horn: short end of the stick

Grum: gloomy

Hang up the fiddle: give up

Hoister: manipulator, operator

Hornswoggle: cheat

Humbugs: deceptions

Knock into a cocked hat: to knock senseless

Necktie sociable: hanging

Pucker: state of irritation

Puke: A person from Missouri

Right smart: a large quantity

Rip-snortin': An impressive person

Saw the elephant: see it all clearly

sharper: a crook

Shut pan: shut up

Swan: swear

Wake snakes: raise a ruckus

Wrathy: to be angry

CHAPTER ONE

Yesterday, 1983

The woman in the photo inside the ornate silver frame appeared flushed, happy. It had been taken near the pond and the surface sparkled in the background, the perfect setting for a man and a woman beginning their future together. A pair of white swans swam across the sparkling water, the symbolism of their presence not being lost on Celeste.

Swans mate for life.

She picked up the brush on the makeup table and started brushing her long, brown hair, thinking about her future and wondering what it would be like. It would be vastly different from the life she was currently living. She knew that without a doubt.

And she'd be free of Him.

Celeste brushed the silky strands away from her round face, her hazel gaze sparking with pleasure at the realization that she would finally realize her childhood dreams, humble though they were, with the man she loved.

The thought brought another on its heels. A much darker one. But Celeste pushed it away, her gaze sliding toward the antique wedding dress she'd pulled from a trunk in the attic.

Celeste had found the dress when she was a child. She'd always loved to play in the crowded attic where it had been stored, reveling in the feeling that she'd traveled to a simpler and much more romantic time.

The attic room was filled to the brim with stuff from what had seemed, to the little girl at least, like ancient times. And everything she'd touched had seemed to warm under the weight of that history, leaving a residue of romance behind in the dust coating her childish fingers.

Celeste had found the dress wrapped carefully in delicate, yellowed paper, its ivory silk loveliness calling to her as she reached carefully to slide a finger over its rich drapes. The bodice was covered in tiny seed pearls. The shoulders dropped, draping over the tops of the wearer's arms in elegant folds. There was a matching pair of gloves, which would have come well above the lucky bride's elbows, tied at the top by ivory silk bows that were threaded through the delicate fabric.

There was a crown of carefully embroidered flowers and a veil that would trail well behind the wife-to-be on the floor.

And beneath it all, a dainty pair of ivory slippers whose toes were covered with tiny, matching pearls.

At that moment, her eyes sparkling in anticipation of the possibilities, Celeste had vowed to herself that she would wear the beautiful wedding gown one day. And it would be the happiest day of her life.

Her hazel gaze in the mirror turned wistful.

Her wedding would be perfect. She would be stunning in her antique dress. And her husband... Celeste sighed.

He would hold her close and dance with her for hours after the wedding. He would whisper words of love in her ear.

Doubt threaded its way through her beautiful thoughts. An ugly truth tugged against her hopes.

Celeste's eyes went dark in the mirror. Her lips thinned under the harsh reminder. There were challenges she still needed to address. People who needed to be brought around.

Mother for one. She'd made her feelings all too clear. And the other. The one who truly stood between Celeste and her dreams.

That one would need to be dealt with.

Celeste saw the door to her room opening in the mirror and turned, her eyes wide in expectation. She wasn't surprised by the figure who moved through the door, eyes fixed with determination on the expectant face.

"Has it been taken care of?" She asked, trying not to sound too hopeful.

The figure frowned, then gave a quick shake of the head. "Not yet."

Celeste squelched her disappointment. "I see."

The figure moved closer, expression severe. "There's still time. It will be all right. I promise."

She forced a smile. "I know. I trust you. But you promise it will be soon?"

The figure reached out, touched her chin with one, long finger. "You have my word."

It took Celeste a moment to understand when the hand wrapped around her throat. Tightened. The face behind the hands going dark with deadly intent.

Her eyes bulged from fear as she struggled against the grip, trying to breathe. Her nails clawed at the gloves she hadn't noticed until that moment.

The gaze held hers, filled with rage and hate.

The room darkened as the fingers tightened just that much more, and she felt her body fold upon itself as death took her into its chilly embrace.

And the last thing she heard was the once-trusted voice, filled with venom. "*Now* it's taken care of Miss Cele. You're where you're supposed to be at last."

She tried to shake her head, her lips moving to speak the words she would never get a chance to utter. *Not me!* Her mind screamed in silent horror. *It wasn't supposed to be me.*

But in the end, it was.

Present Day

"Will you two *please* stop fighting?" Anna scoured a look from her employee and boyfriend, Pratt Davies to the grayish-white figure standing nearby, the occasional blipping of his form not doing anything to hide the glower on his handsome face as he shoved the cowboy hat back on his head and dropped his arms into gunslinger stance.

Anna rolled her eyes. "You're both right. Now can we stop this arguing, please? The sooner we get this task done, the sooner we can get out of here."

Anna fixed a stern look on each of her favorite men, one at a time, and waited until they nodded before looking away. "Good. I've already got the willies and we're not even inside yet."

Pratt frowned. "If you want to wait in the car…"

She turned the old-fashioned key in the ancient lock of the front door and lifted her brows. "I'm fine. I can't think of anything more boring than sitting in a car all day. Besides, you'll need me to tell you what to tag for the shop and what to mark for disposal."

"I reckon it's better to be bored than dead, darlin'," Joss told her while glaring at Pratt.

She sighed. "Look. I know it's too soon for us to be heading back into another haunted mansion. I get it. We're all on edge. But this opportunity was just too great to pass up. And Old Mrs. Dashery has no other heirs. She wanted me to have this stuff for *Yesterday's Antiques*."

"I've seen what's inside," Pratt said, glaring right back at Joss. "This is an epic opportunity. She has some incredible antiques in this big old house."

"You already said that, Puke. But there's enough spirit'al activity in this house to wake snakes. My skin's crawlin' with it. It don't make sense to put Miss Anna in danger again so soon. None of us has recovered from the last time."

The *last time*, had been a Christmas party at their friend Duncan Nelson's big old home. Duncan's family had long been acquainted with the spooks in his historic home. But unfortunately for all, there was at least one ghost he hadn't known was there. And that one nearly cost them all their lives.

"It's fine, Joss. This was my idea, not Pratt's. I want to do this."

The cowboy finally expelled air he didn't really breathe and scratched the dark gold hair under his hat. "Okay, darlin'. But I'm stickin' to you like paraffin until we get out of there."

Anna gave him a smile. "I'm counting on it."

"I think you mean glue," Pratt said.

"Huh?"

"You're sticking to her like glue, not wax."

"Shut pan, Puke. I've had about as much of your nonsense as I can stomach."

Anna pushed the door open and was immediately assailed by a cool breeze laden with dust. She sneezed, barely noticing the continued bickering behind her as she looked around. The entryway was wide, the ceiling high, with a massive window along the top that was streaked with mud on the outside and improper cleaning on the inside. Though it was messy, with mud streaking the elegant black marble floors, and the dust and detritus left behind by the police and medical personnel, Anna could easily picture the stunning beauty it must have once been.

"…Anna?"

She blinked and turned, realizing Pratt had been speaking to her. "I'm sorry, I was just taking it all in."

He grinned. "Wait until you see the tin ceiling in the kitchen."

Anna felt a surge of excitement at the thought. The tin would fetch a pretty penny, either purchased in total or in separate sections as wall decorations. Although, she hated to pull them down and deface the beautiful old home. She and

Pratt had been "discussing" that very thing for days and hadn't yet managed to come up with a solution that made both of them happy. Of course, he worked for her so he'd do whatever she wanted. But she liked to keep him happy when she could. His opinion was important to her. Also, she didn't want to revive the argument again. "I can't wait to see it."

She pointed to the marble-topped table in the center of the entryway. "That will come with us."

Pratt nodded and jotted a quick description of the location and appearance in a notebook he'd brought for that purpose. Then he snapped a picture of it with his cell phone.

Anna walked over to a massive, mahogany-framed mirror that hung on yellowed, rose-covered wallpaper on the side wall. She ran a fingertip over the intricately carved frame. "Stunning," she murmured to herself.

Pratt stepped up beside her, "This must weigh two hundred pounds."

She nodded. "Easily. Add it to the list."

"Yes, ma'am."

They shared a smile and Anna pointed to the matching cabinet below the mirror. "This too."

An hour later they were working their way through the library when Anna's head came up. An icy breeze slipped over her and her breath came out in little puffs of fog. "Pratt?"

He was carefully noting down the titles of the books they'd selected from the bookshelves that encompassed an entire wall, and was barely paying attention to her. "Mm-hmm?"

"Where's Joss?"

Pratt didn't seem to hear. "Did you know this one was a first edition?" His handsome face held a reverence Anna would have enjoyed had her spidey senses not been clanging. "Pratt!"

His head jerked around and he frowned. "What's wrong?" Then he noted the fog leaving his mouth and moved quickly to his feet. "Where is it?"

Anna assumed he meant the ghost that had joined them in the library. She shook her head. "I'm worried about Joss. I just realized we haven't seen or heard from him since we entered the house."

"He's probably just off pouting somewhere."

"I do not pout, Puke."

Anna whipped around, laughing nervously. "There you go sneaking up on me again, Joss."

"Boo!"

They shared a smile, the joke an old favorite between them.

"What did you find?" Pratt asked the ghost.

Joss frowned, but didn't get a chance to respond before a second figure eased into view. The ghost was dressed in clothing from Joss' era but he was clearly not a cowboy. He looked more like a businessman or a...

"Gambler," Joss murmured, seeming as always to read her mind. "This here's Josiah Baumgartner," Joss told her, his mouth twisting over the name as if it left a sour taste on his tongue. "A hoister and a grifter. He'll hornswoggle ya as soon as look at ya. Watch yourself with this one, darlin'."

Anna remembered when Joss had said much the same about Pratt, when he'd come unexpectedly into their lives. Her ghostly friend had been dead wrong then. But looking at the smug haughtiness in the handsome lines of the new ghost's face, Anna doubted Joss was exaggerating. "Mr. Baumgartner. How are you?"

The man was sprawled in a walnut Queen Anne chair from the 1700s, one leg bent over a delicate arm and the other stretched out before him, an appropriately named Gambler style top hat lying across his knee. "I'm better now that you're here, Ma'am."

"Don't try to sweet talk Miss Anna, hound dog. I'll beat ya into the last century if you so much as look at her sideways."

Baumgartner's dark gaze flashed with annoyance. "I don't want to hornswoggle anybody, you uncouth coot. I'm just here to ask for some help."

Anna gave Joss a quelling look. Despite her friend's warnings, she had to admit she was curious. "What do you need help with, Mr. Baumgartner?"

With a final glare at Joss, Josiah Baumgartner unfolded his long form from the chair and bowed, his hat pressed against his broad chest. "Pleased to make your acquaintance Miss Anna. The ether is filled with stories about you and your…" His lip curled as he scoured a look over Pratt and Joss.

Both of her protectors had moved closer, ready to jump in if she needed them.

"…associates," Baumgartner finished.

"It is, is it?" Anna didn't like the sound of that.

"Yes, ma'am. All good, I assure you. I've been informed that you are an advocate of sorts for the spiritual world."

"Only for those who deserve it," Pratt growled out.

Anna could feel the tension rolling off him in waves. She reached out and clasped his hand. "I help if I can, yes."

"Well that's fortuitous. Because I am greatly in need of your assistance, Miss Anna."

"With *what*, man!" Joss roared. "Get to the dang point." The lights in the library flickered under his wrath and ice formed on the chairs.

"The *point*, Mr. Zebediah, is that I'd like to leave this place and find my proper spot up high. But I cannot. Because that addlepated old woman hid my bones from me."

CHAPTER TWO

Anna didn't quite know where to start. There were so many questions suddenly in her mind. But she decided to begin with the obvious. "What addle…" She cleared her throat. "What old woman would that be?"

"Why the lady of the house, of course." His handsome visage darkened in a glower. "The one who's since joined me in the ether."

Which presented another question.

Pratt beat her to it. "If she's there in the ether, why don't you just ask her where your bones are."

"If only it were that simple, my good sir."

"Stop your wiles, snake," Joss snapped. "He ain't nobody's good sir."

Pratt gave Joss an uncertain look, clearly wondering if that was a shot.

Anna hid a smile. She was pretty sure it was meant to be Joss' attempt at a defense. When push came to shove, the two of them usually stood up for each other. Though they generally fought like cats and dogs. "It seems like a reasonable question," Anna offered.

"I reckon it does," Baumgartner agreed pleasantly. "But the woman was quite addlepated when she was alive. She's of a right mind now but she can't recall what she did when she was in that state." He shook his head, frowning.

She'd heard stories about Mrs. Dashery's mental issues. It had been rumored she was suffering from dementia. Anna had been concerned that the old woman's will would be disputed because of her mental condition and had spoken to the lawyer about it. Fortunately, or unfortunately for poor Mrs. Dashery, no one had been able to discover any living relatives, so there was no one to dispute it. Her only daughter had been murdered thirty-some years earlier, long before Mrs. Dashery had been rumored to begin showing signs of dementia. "She'd been ill, I understand."

"Yes, ma'am. So, you see I need your help. If I could find 'em myself I surely would. But I don't have the kind of spiritual gunpowder to move physical objects. Not easily or quickly."

"What's your hurry? You got nothin' but time, hoister," Joss mused unhelpfully.

"Joss…"

He spared Anna a quick glance, his frown softening. "Don't waste your pity on this scoundrel, darlin'. I knew him when he walked the earth and I doubt he's any less of a grifter now than he was when he was alive."

Amazingly, Baumgartner nodded. "He's telling you the absolute truth, ma'am. I was a scoundrel when I lived. I freely admit it. But death has a way of clarifying one's views on things. You have my word…" When Joss bristled, Baumgartner lifted a hand to stop him from commenting. "On my saintly mother's grave… I mean no harm to anyone here. I merely wish to join my beloved in the place of light and peace."

Joss snickered. "Only thing you ever *beloved* was cash."

Baumgartner frowned. "You haven't known me for a long time, cowboy."

Anna lifted a hand to cut into the quarrel she could see escalating. "I don't see what harm there would be in looking for Mr. Baumgartner's lost bones while we take inventory."

She slid a questioning glance toward Pratt. He didn't look happy about it but he nodded. "As long as it doesn't require us to tear down walls."

"Spectacular!" Baumgartner's smile was wide and filled with excitement. He rubbed ghostly hands together and started to dim. "I'll just get out of your way then. I trust the cowboy can let me know if…when…you find them?"

Anna didn't dare look at Joss. She could feel his disapproval in the frosty air. "We'll find a way to let you know, Mr. Baumgartner." She gave the spirit a smile and he bowed, snapping away and taking some of the frigid temps with him when he left.

Unfortunately, there was still enough frost in the room to turn Anna's breath to fog.

"I wish you'd trust my judgment, darlin'."

She shook her head. "It's not that I don't trust you, Joss. But Mr. Baumgartner hasn't harmed anyone here and doesn't show any signs of intending to do so. If that changes we'll deal with him. But the truth is, if his bones are holding him in this house, we're stuck with him either way. We might as well try to keep things civil."

Joss frowned but didn't argue. He stood with arms crossed over a wide chest, the brim of his cowboy hat shading his gaze. "I'll keep an eye on the sharper." He disappeared without another word and Anna rubbed her arms, glad for the removal of her friend's blustery disapproval. She lifted her brows at Pratt and he chuckled.

"Back to work," he said, pointing toward another wall full of books. "I think this library will take us all day to sort through."

"You're right. But there seem to be a lot of valuable books in here. It doesn't make sense to rush it."

"What do you want to do with the books that aren't worth anything?" he asked as he settled back down in front of the pile of books he'd been sorting.

"They're books, Pratt."

He glanced up at the sharp tone of her voice and she grinned. "*Every* book is worth something. A few are just worth more than others."

He shook his head, chuckling.

"Denise is part owner of that used bookstore downtown. We'll give her first chance at them and anything that's left we'll donate."

"I didn't realize that."

Denise Block was Anna's best friend, a well-known author of a bestselling series of children's books. Denise had also recently discovered the spiritual plane and its inhabitants. Anna wasn't sure how her friend was taking her newfound knowledge of ghosts, but at least Anna no longer had to hide Joss or her other resident ghost, Bess', presence from her friend.

It was a huge relief.

"She bought in last year. A few months after you came to Crocker. I didn't think to mention it." Anna settled down at the desk in the middle of the room and tugged on the center drawer. It opened to show some elderly pens, several bent paper clips, a few chewed pencils and a lot of dust. She opened the top drawer on one side and found a bunch of old greeting cards. Glancing through them, she realized they were from Mrs. Dashery's daughter Celeste. It made her sad to watch the childish scrawl of the first few, homemade cards filled with construction paper confetti and glitter, turn into the elegant script of a young woman and realize Mrs. Dashery lost her only child much too early. Judging by the flowery and impersonal messages on the cards and the coolness of the written signatures, Anna could only assume the two women had not been close.

A strange feeling of sadness washed through her. The emotion felt foreign, too intense to be her own and she shivered under its impact. Anna laid the pile of cards on top of the desk. She had no idea what she was going to do with them. It didn't feel right to throw them away. But they were of no use to anyone outside the Dashery family and there didn't seem to be anything left of the lineage.

Another wave of sadness swamped her. Anna sat back in the chair, her body turning icy and her gaze blank. She had only an instant to become alarmed before it hit her…the brief, violent vision was like a punch to the gut.

A hostile gaze, squinting with dark intent, and a fearful cry, as disembodied hands snaked out from the fog and grasped her around the throat. She tried to scream but the ghostly grip choked off the sound. The pressure built, causing her eyes to bulge and her head to pound as panic seared through her. She reached up, tried to grip the ghostly hands at her throat, but her fingers slipped through the fog, finding nothing solid to grip.

Unfortunately, the pressure on her throat was very real.

Anna struggled against a deep lethargy and the bone-chilling cold. Something tugged at her arms and a deep, worried voice called her name. The pressure at her throat eased and she felt herself sagging downward, but the cold still infused her bones and the feeling of being lost in the fog was terrifying.

It had to be ether.

How was that possible?

Anna's gaze slowly lifted to watch a slender, dark figure walk away, its form hidden inside a floor-length, hooded cloak and the blustery mist…

"Anna! Anna, wake up! What's happening?"

A small part of her recognized Pratt's terrified question, but Anna couldn't pull herself free. She watched that retreating form, her mind struggling to recognize her killer.

Ice crept through her body, slowing the beating of her heart. She could almost feel her blood turning to sludge in her veins. Her thoughts turning fuzzy.

The figure in the swirling fog stopped, started to turn, and a hate-filled gaze pierced the ether, hitting her with the force of a blow.

Why? She asked the figure, watching the cruel lips curve upward.

You shouldn't have done it…Celeste.

Anna frowned. *But I'm not…*

The world spun and a familiar force slammed into her, sending her flying backward, toward a warm glow of light that beckoned her from the ether. She hit the light and it was like a thousand shards of glass ripping through her flesh.

When she came back to consciousness, Pratt had her in his arms and they were seated on the floor, in front of a smoky fire that was just starting to show tendrils of flame in the long-unused fireplace. Anna forced the terrifying experience away and focused on Pratt's arms, wrapped around her, the heat of the fire, and the musty smelling blanket he'd covered her with.

But as her mind returned inexorably to that murky place of fear and violence, Anna didn't think she'd ever be completely warm again.

"Are you okay?" Pratt asked. His big hands still rubbed up and down her arms as Anna came back to herself and fought the chill permeating her body. "I think so." She shook her head and straightened away from him, though the loss of his warmth was like a physical blow.

Shivering violently, Anna pushed to her feet. "That was pretty disturbing."

"What happened?" he asked. Pratt stood too, staying close, his hands lifted in her direction as if he thought she might fall and he'd have to catch her.

Anna shook her head. "I wish I knew. One minute I was looking at those cards…" Her gaze fell on the scattered cards littering the floor around the desk. "I had a flash of…something."

"Flash? Like a premonition?" Pratt frowned. He was no stranger to paranormal things, but his initiation into the world of spirits and ether had been so traumatic that whenever they encountered something new his first reaction was resistance, with a side of barely controlled terror.

After hearing the story of his St. Louis experience, when he'd been a cop, she could understand why. "Not a premonition, no." She thought about it for a moment, trying to capture the feeling that had overwhelmed her. "I guess it was more like a memory. It was as if I'd stepped into another time…" She shuddered again.

"Well, that's new."

She glanced his way, taking note of the worry in his sexy gaze, and felt the sudden need to reassure them both. There was only one way to do that which didn't involve donuts and coffee. Anna stepped into his arms and allowed herself to be comforted, knowing it would comfort him as well. Her eyes closed as his reassuring warmth surrounded her and she sighed. "I'm sure it was nothing. I'm just worked up about being here so soon after…"

Pratt stiffened slightly. "I hate to say it but I'm starting to worry that Joss was right. Maybe it's just too soon for us to be doing this."

Anna shook her head. "Not a chance. I'm fine." She gave him a smile to prove it. But even *she* could tell it was just a stiff bending of her lips. There was no genuine pleasure in it. "Let's get back to work."

"No. You need to sit in front of this fire for a few minutes. Let me finish going through these books and then we'll go have some lunch."

Anna had to admit lunch sounded good. "Sounds like a plan. But I'm not going to sit on my butt while you work. I'll finish up with the desk."

He shook his head. "Stubborn woman."

Anna dropped into a crouch to pick up the cards she'd dropped. The floor around them was covered in construction paper confetti and it made Anna sad. When she had them all gathered up, she slipped them back into the drawer where she'd found them and closed it, her hand resting for a moment on the knob.

What had she experienced? It had felt like an attack. An attack on Celeste Dashery. Anna frowned. Had she relived the other woman's murder?

Anna looked around, wondering what it must have been like for Mrs. Dashery to continue living in the home after the murder. It had been the Dashery family's home for their entire lives. Yet it had to have taken on a different feel after Celeste was gone.

Anna's gaze lifted toward the ceiling. When Anna had been informed of the contents of Mrs. Dashery's will, the lawyer had given her a packet of papers. Inside the packet was a hand-drawn accounting of the rooms in the big house and the furnishings of worth within each of them.

She remembered Celeste's room. It was on the second level, pretty much right above their heads. "I want to tackle the daughter's room after lunch," she told Pratt.

He glanced up briefly, nodding. "That works for me. There was a Louis the Eighth style makeup table in that room that I wanted to check out."

Anna's gaze was locked on the ceiling, her body trembling as waves of cold seemed to reach toward her from above. "Yes," she said softly. "I want to see that table too."

But mostly she wanted to see it because it had starred in the vision or memory or whatever it was she'd just experienced.

And Anna had a terrible feeling it had been the site of much more than Celeste Dashery's beautifying rituals.

CHAPTER THREE

Sitting across the table from Anna at their favorite Italian restaurant, Pratt watched her carefully, not at all surprised she wasn't eating the meatball sub in front of her. She hadn't spoken three words since he'd coerced her into leaving the mansion. They'd brought sandwiches in a cooler for lunch, but Pratt wanted to get her out of that place for a while.

She was too pale. And when she reached for her iced tea he couldn't miss the way her hand trembled.

"I think we should call it a day," he said again, determined to plow through her resistance to the idea.

She shook her head, fixing a haunted look on him. "I have to go back."

Not "want" to go back. "Have" to go back, he mused. Something was up. He eyed her, unsure whether he should simply insist. But despite her pale unsteadiness, her resolve seemed unshakable. "Not unless you can tell me why?"

She spun the glass holding her iced tea, her pretty blue gaze locked on it. She frowned slightly, as if she didn't like her own thoughts. "I can't explain it. I just have to go up to Celeste's room."

He leaned across the table, forcing her gaze to skim to his. "I hate to admit this, honey, but I'm afraid the Cowboy was right. It was a bad idea to go into a mansion we knew had ghosts. You haven't had enough time to heal…"

"Bull."

He blinked in surprise. "What?"

"You're fine. You suffered as much if not more than I did at Duncan's."

He frowned. "That's not the point…"

She finally really looked at him, some of the vagueness leaving her gaze. "It's exactly the point. I wasn't targeted in that house. It had something to do with those cards I was holding. But now that I've gotten a glimpse of Celeste's death I realize that I need to find out what happened to her and why." She gave him a gentle smile, reaching across to clasp his hand.

Her fingers were icy.

"I promise it will be okay. I'll have you and Joss with me. If whatever it was finds me again, I'll be ready for it."

He sat back, sighing in defeat. "Okay, but at the first sign you're in trouble we're hightailing it out of that house and you're not going back. Agree?"

She agreed much too readily. Without seeming to consider his words.

In fact, it seemed a lot like she had no intention of honoring the quick promise implied by the nod of her head.

~SC~

The hallway outside Celeste Dashery's bedroom was cold enough for their breath to fog the air. Despite her brave words to Pratt, Anna was terrified. She never wanted to feel the helplessness of that previous visitation again.

Celeste Dashery had been murdered right before Anna's eyes. Yet Anna couldn't offer one single detail about the killer. It was all cloaked in mist. Except for the eyes. Anna thought she'd have nightmares about the hate in those dark eyes for the rest of her life.

Pratt reached out and clasped her hand. "Are you sure?"

Anna tried to speak but the words wouldn't emerge from her throat. She finally settled for a nod.

"Well I ain't," Joss grumbled. "Only a coot'd go into a place that's filled with haunts. I'm one o' them haunts and even I'm feelin' all-overish about this place."

Anna shook her head. "You're just being overprotective, Joss." But the smile she gave him was tighter than she'd have liked. "If both of you stay close to me I'll be fine."

Pratt frowned at Joss. "Where's your buddy? Do you think he had a hand in what happened earlier?"

Joss shoved his hat back off his forehead. Deep lines of worry creased the spot between his dark blue eyes. "I wouldn't put nothin' past that scoundrel. But I don't feel him here now."

Pratt jerked his head toward the door. "Why don't you go on ahead and check out the room."

He gave Joss a look that had Anna's temper rising. "Will you two stop it. I'll be fine." Saying the words *did* make her feel better. In fact, she reached for the doorknob and, before Pratt could stop her, turned it, flinging the door open.

A strident hiss sounded from inside the room and something skittered toward them, sending alarm bells clanging in Anna's chest.

She felt her eyes go wide and she screamed before she could stop herself.

The low-slung brown critter shot past her feet and disappeared with an angry sound into a hole in the wall behind a dresser.

Anna folded into Pratt, her heart pounding.

Her protectors both eyed her with raised brows and humor shining in their eyes.

She laughed and it felt good, releasing a boatload of pent-up tension. "I guess we need to add an exterminator to the list of things we need to do to sell the house."

Pratt let his lips curve upward. "I don't know. That was a pretty big rat. We might need to call in a big game hunter."

She laughed again, shaking her head. "Okay, let's do this."

The deep chill in the air of Celeste's bedroom dissipated fairly quickly. Whatever had been there when they arrived seemed to have left. Anna told herself it had just been their ghostly host, Josiah, playing games, but she was having trouble fully convincing herself.

A cold that brittle and deep was generally only found around a poltergeist type spook.

Anna frowned at the thought. There were two things that terrified her about that idea. One, they didn't need to bump up against any more raging spirits. They'd had their fill of those the Christmas before. And, two, a spirit *that* angry had to be the victim of murder or extreme violence.

Which meant Celeste Dashery was probably still haunting the bedroom where she was killed.

Awesome.

Anna soon forgot her concerns as she and Pratt cataloged the furnishings in the room. The bedroom set appeared handmade and hand-carved, the glossy posts of the canopy bed standing over seven feet tall. The satin fabric draping the posts, though dusty and yellowed slightly with time, was edged with rare and expensive handmade lace.

"That's beautiful," Pratt said over her shoulder as she fingered the yellowed lace. "What is it?"

"They call it bobbin or pillow lace. You don't see it much anymore. Lace is mostly made by machine now."

"That should be worth something."

Anna dropped the fabric and sighed, looking around. "I'm starting to worry we won't have room for everything in the shop."

"That's a concern for sure. We'll have to store some of it."

"It will have to be someplace temperature controlled. I don't know where that would be off the top of my head."

"Maybe Vance would know of someplace. Or maybe he'd have room to store it for us."

Her eyes went wide. "That's a great idea. I could pay him rent for the space. I figure he could use a little extra income."

The *Bickershaw Museum* was located in downtown Crocker, near the edge of the small town. It had once been the family home of its current owner's wealthy ancestors. There was a rocky story behind the place, and the old mansion had ghosts of its own, both figuratively and possibly literally, but Vance Bickershaw had been working hard to make it a "must see" spot in Crocker. "I'll call him tonight." She gave Pratt a kiss on the cheek. "You're a genius."

His grin made her stomach flip with pleasure. "Thanks, beautiful."

"If you two are done with the disgustin' displays of affection…"

They looked around as Joss popped into view, more than his presence frosty. His glare toward Pratt was downright glacial. "We're just about done here for the day, Joss," Anna told him to distract him from his pique. "Everything okay in the ether?"

Joss' glare turned to a thoughtful frown. "Not by half. I'll be right chirk to be quit of this place." He strode across the room, his gaze locked onto Anna with an intensity he usually reserved for the times he was warning her away from Pratt.

Not that he'd had much success on that recently.

Or ever.

"How about you take my advice and hang up the fiddle on this place, darlin'. I got a bad feelin' about it."

Anna's fingers itched to reach out and touch his arm, to give him reassurance. But the touch would be far from pleasant for either of them. Unless one longed for the days of electric shock treatments. "It's fine, Joss. You worry too much."

He shook his head and threw one last glare at Pratt as if everything that was wrong in his world was the other man's fault.

Anna figured that was exactly how Joss felt. "I just want to give the makeup table a quick search and then we're out of here."

Joss inclined his chin. "I'll make another sweep through the house and meet ya by the door."

He popped away and Pratt sighed. "He sure worries a lot."

Anna sat down in front of the small, curved table and looked at Pratt's handsome reflection in the mirror. "He sees things you and I don't."

"Yeah. But you'd think a dead guy would be braver."

Anna's lips twitched on a smile. "I don't doubt he's right about this place." She shivered before she could stop herself. "It has a strange vibe. I'll admit I'll be happy when we're out of here."

She pulled the center drawer open and squealed.

Pratt was there immediately as she shoved the chair away from the desk. Anna put a hand over her chest and laughed, the sound breathy as her heart pounded hard. "Dang, that about scared the life out of me."

Pratt reached past her, his fingers clasping the object sitting atop some kind of journal. "It looks like we found our first piece of Mr. Baumgartner."

He held it up between them and they examined it. "Is that a finger bone?"

"Looks like. What do you want me to do with it?"

Anna frowned. "I hadn't thought about that. I guess we'll put it somewhere here, in the house. But not in the furniture."

"The Butler's pantry off the kitchen?"

She nodded. "Perfect." She made quick work of the makeup table and stepped back. "Nothing else of interest in this thing."

"Do you want to take the table?" Pratt asked. He had his pen hovering over the notebook he'd been cataloging items into all day.

She thought about it for a beat and then shook her head. "No. I don't think so. It's not in very good shape and it's cheaply made." She frowned. "I'm actually surprised. Everything else in this room is valuable."

"Maybe Celeste bought it with her own money."

"Yeah. Could be." Anna considered the hand-decorated journal she'd placed on top of the makeup table. She wanted to read through it to get a feel for Celeste's life at Dashery House. But she was more than ready to get out of there. A hot meal and an even hotter shower were calling to her.

After a moment's consideration she grabbed the diary, planning to take it home with her to examine that night. She smiled at Pratt. "Ready?"

"I've never been so ready."

Anna was feeling pretty good about their day's work as she stepped out into the hallway. Her day got even better as Pratt dropped an arm around her shoulders and pulled her close.

It took a giant dive downward though, at the shrill scream that rose up to them from the first floor as they started to descend.

CHAPTER FOUR

The young woman was cowering against the closed front door, her arms outstretched and her hands raised in a classic attempt to hold something back. Only there was nothing to hold back.

Unless she counted one very perplexed-looking cowboy from the 1800s and his ex-best-friend the hoister. They stood staring at the pale-faced girl, seemingly uncertain how to respond.

Clearly, she could see them. Or at least see something of them, even if it was just a thickening of the air, or the icy residue ghosts sometimes left behind on furniture and walls.

Anna hurried down the stairs, catching Joss' eye and giving him a smile. "Hello." She stuck her hand out and approached the young woman, who looked to be in her early twenties. For a moment Anna was afraid the woman would ignore her hand and continue bracing the admittedly cold air in front of her with her hands.

But she finally risked a quick look Anna's way. "You don't…see them?"

Well, that answered that. "Them?" Anna wasn't about to give anything away she didn't have to. The last thing she wanted to do was surprise the young intruder into fainting dead away in the entryway.

"Those…" She flicked her fingers at Joss. He frowned, scratching his head and shoving his cowboy hat back on his head. "Spirits." She said the word with such distaste that even Josiah Baumgartner seemed to find it within his cynical heart to be offended. "Now see here, Miss…"

The girl yelped, jumping another foot farther away. One, pale hand with slender fingers tipped in perfect cotton candy pink polish clutched the knob. "Don't you come any closer. I'm wearing a cross."

As she said the words her free hand pressed against her flat chest, indicating that the fearful object was hidden beneath her lightweight sweater.

Joss eyed her, his handsome face folding into a frown. "Now don't you go all skeery on us, Miss. Josiah's a grifter but far as I know he ain't a vampire."

The grifter snorted out a laugh. "'Tis true. I've been known to drain a spinster or two of their coin. But I have no taste for blood."

The girl blinked at them and then turned to look a question at Anna.

"They're harmless," Anna assured her. Then she smiled. "Mostly."

A soft gasp told her the girl hadn't taken to her small joke. "I'm kidding." She offered her hand again. "I'm Anna Yesterday."

The girl finally took Anna's offering, giving her hand a limp pump before dropping it. She kept a wary look on the two ghosts, only skimming it quickly away when Pratt came up beside Anna. "Pratt Davies." She took his offered hand a lot more readily, and she gave him a come-hither smile to go with it. "Pleased to meet you, Pratt."

"That's Joss and Josiah," Anna offered. "They're friendly."

"Like Casper the Friendly Ghost," Pratt offered, grinning.

Joss glared over at him.

The young woman didn't look convinced. "You know them?"

"I know Joss." Anna agreed. "He's my friend. And he vouches for Mr. Baumgartner."

"I did no such thing," Joss grumbled. "But I ain't known him ta harm the ladies."

"Only their purses," Josiah said with an unrepentant grin. He stood up from where he'd been lounging in the usual chair and bowed deeply. "At your service, Miss."

"What can we help you with?" Anna asked, offering a smile to take the sting out of her question.

The young woman blinked in surprise. "I…well I…I came to see to Grandmother's things."

Anna shared a look with Pratt.

"Can you clarify that, please?" Pratt asked. "Who is your grandmother and what things are you here to see?"

The girl finally smiled. "I'm sorry. I'm being rude. It's just that those two threw me off a bit."

Anna chuckled. "I can certainly understand that."

The girl frowned toward the two ghosts again. She was undoubtedly uncomfortable with their presence but she looked confused too. She'd probably never seen a ghost, let alone met two people who weren't surprised they were there. She seemed to shake it off after a moment. "I'm Agatha Miller. My grandmother was Celeste Dashery's governess and, later, the housekeeper."

Anna smiled. "Oh, how nice. Is she still alive?"

The woman nodded. "Very much so. But she has bad hips these days and doesn't get around very well. She sent me to deal with the house."

Anna felt a disturbing tightness in her belly. "This house? But…"

She wasn't sure how to tell the young woman that the house didn't belong to Mrs. Miller. It seemed rude to just come right out with it.

Joss had no such compunction. "Your grandma don't own this house, Miss Miller. Miss Anna does. Old Mrs. Dashery left it to her."

The young woman's brown eyes went very wide. "Oh, but that's not true. We have the paperwork to prove it. Mrs. Dashery left the house to Grandma for her years of faithful service."

Anna's spirits fell. She'd known it was too good to be true. "I guess we have a problem then. I have paperwork that says she left it all to me."

"But why would she do that?" Agatha asked, her forehead crinkling in a frown.

"Her will said she wanted her things to be cared for and she trusted me to make sure they would be." Anna shook her head. "There's clearly been some kind of misunderstanding. I'm sure we can work it out."

Agatha's pretty face darkened with anger. "Yes, we certainly will. And in the meantime, I suggest you stay off my grandmother's property. And I'll need to search that truck outside to make sure you haven't already hauled some of it off."

Anna bit back an angry response, forcing herself to speak slowly and calmly. "I'm afraid it's you who have the burden of proof in this, Agatha. I have a legal document that says I'm the owner of Dashery Cottage. Where is your legal document?"

"I. Well, I don't have it on me. Grandmother has it."

Anna nodded. "Well, then if she does have such a thing…"

"Of course she does. Are you calling me a liar?"

"If she does, then you'll need to get a lawyer and have it analyzed for authenticity."

Pratt stepped forward and pulled the door open. "Have a nice day, Miss Miller."

The girl puffed up like an angry cat and glared around the room. Her face turned an alarming shade of red. Finally, she expelled an angry huff of air. "Fine. I'll go. But I'll be back.

And I'll bring the police with me the next time. To throw you off my...our property."

They watched her stomp outside and down the steps, toward a small, light blue car that was sitting just behind Pratt's recently purchased truck.

Pratt closed the door and they shared a look.

Anna shook her head, dropping into the chair Josiah had abandoned. "This is all I need."

"You want I should put the spectral whoop ass on her the next time she comes, darlin'?"

Anna shook her head. "Tempting. But no. We need to resolve this legally. In the meantime, we can keep cataloging but let's not remove anything from the house. Just in case."

Pratt nodded toward the diary she still held. "Including that?"

Anna looked down. "I'll bring it back in the morning. But I want to read it tonight. Maybe I can make some sense out of what happened to me earlier."

It occurred to Anna that skittish Miss Agatha might not be so thrilled with the house if she'd experienced what Anna had in the library. She almost smiled at the thought. Then she felt guilty for it. Whatever she'd accidentally bumped up against by touching those homemade cards, it had felt dangerous and threatening.

However annoying Agatha Miller seemed, Anna wouldn't wish a repeat of that experience on anyone.

~SC~

Anna stood on the sidewalk outside of *The Finishing Touch*, funeral parlor and home decorating store, and waved as Pratt's truck pulled away. Before he'd driven her home, they'd taken Joss back to *Yesterday's Antiques* and Anna had made a quick call to her lawyer.

She'd left a message with Connie Dung of *Dung, Sabin and Roth*, the sole group of lawyers Crocker could boast, and tried to push the problem to the back of her mind. There was nothing she could do about it until the lawyers hashed things out. Walking around with a lead balloon in her belly wasn't going to help.

She needed to de-stress.

Anna turned toward the metal staircase attached to the side of the building and started climbing toward her cozy little apartment on the second floor. High above her head, a long, low rumble of thunder rolled through the sky and the first fat drops of rain pinged off the canopy overhead. Anna inhaled the smell of the coming rain, enjoying the brisk wind that sent the edges of the canopy dancing.

She loved storms, and the coming rain and overcast skies were a perfect counterpoint to her mood. Though she was trying not to think about the legal tussle ahead, the prospect had left her feeling tired and sad.

She'd known getting ownership of Dashery Cottage was too good to be true.

Anna pulled open the storm door and a piece of paper fluttered out. She bent to pick it up before it blew away. Frowning down at the familiar scrawl, she felt her day go just a little bit darker. Her landlord was raising her rent.

Just perfect.

Anna unlocked her front door and went inside just as the skies opened up. A thunderous downpour pounded onto the roof high above her head. She hung her sweater and purse on the hooks by the door and trudged inside, feeling as if she'd taken a beating.

What she needed was a long, hot bath in her elderly claw foot tub.

That would be just the ticket.

And maybe a glass of wine.

Dropping the journal onto the pass-through counter between her kitchen and the small living room, Anna headed toward the bedroom. She'd have her bath and pull on something warm and soft. And then she'd read the journal until she couldn't keep her eyes open anymore.

It would be a relief to immerse herself in Celeste Dashery's life for a while, and maybe forget some of her own problems.

Two hours later, Anna was rethinking that idea. Reading Celeste's diary was like reading a gothic horror story. The poor girl's life was fraught with bad luck and personal issues.

She was not only a lonely and, by her own accounts, plain-looking woman, but she'd also apparently had trouble all her life fitting in. She had no real friends it seemed, except for the daughter of the governess turned housekeeper. And it appeared that Celeste's mother hadn't exactly been a candidate for mother of the year.

Not that Rebecca Dashery had been cruel or violent. But from Celeste's accounts, her mother had been distant and undemonstrative; her mind caught up in another world.

Remembering the dark presence Anna had felt in the library, she wondered if Mrs. Dashery had been able to see spirits. That would explain her distance. Anna knew from experience how easily one could get enticed by the ether.

There was so much going on there. Danger, intrigue, secrets waiting to be uncovered. Not to mention the spirits themselves. Anna had met all types and she'd learned one thing very quickly.

Just like their living counterparts, they had agendas and weren't to be trusted.

Anna's head shot up as something clattered to the floor at the other end of the small apartment. She closed the journal, sitting very still and listening.

Was that the scrape of a heel on carpet?

Anna pushed the covers back and climbed out of bed. She left the journal there and walked quietly toward her bedroom door.

She stopped in the doorway, listening.

A soft whimper drifted from the darkness beyond the opening. She went very still.

Anna shivered, her breath coming out in soft puffs of frosty air.

Something was in her apartment.

Anna's gaze slid to the phone on her bedside table.

Why hadn't she thought to grab it?

She wondered if she could get to it and dial Pratt before the intruder in the other room was on her. If she was dealing with a supernatural presence as she suspected, it seemed unlikely.

Another whimper brought the hairs up on the back of her neck.

It sounded closer.

Anna stepped slowly backward, her eyes riveted to the darkness beyond the door. Something swirled there. Something hazy and dark, only slightly lighter than the darkness.

She bumped up against her bedside table and stopped, her hand reaching behind to grasp her phone.

Her fingers clutched the cell behind her back, too numb and shaky to dial a number. She pulled air into her lungs on a gasp as the charcoal mist began to take form. The mist swirled and spun, slowly elongating until it stood about five feet five. Then the mist twisted and rounded until a woman stood before her.

The figure stayed outside the glow of Anna's lamp, its dark eyes capturing flecks of the light that turned flat in the dead gaze.

A soft cloud of gray hair lifted around an oblong face. Gray, pasty looking skin bore the tracks of aging, its surface dull and crepey. The form was thick in the middle, with skinny arms and legs decked out in polyester slacks and a white cotton blouse. The blouse was stained and wrinkled, the tiny flowers decorating its surface obscured by a spray of some kind of brown substance.

Anna suddenly realized who it was.

"Mrs. Dashery?"

The figure jerked a bit at the sound of her name, the eyes narrowing slightly. She folded age speckled gray hands in front of her and fixed Anna with a stern look down her short round nose.

"What is it? Do you need to tell me something about the house?"

Rebecca Dashery wavered in the doorway, her wispy form seeming to cringe away from the light, and Anna thought for a beat that the ghost was going to disappear.

But she blinked and Rebecca's arm was suddenly lifting, one bent, arthritic finger pointing toward the bed.

Anna turned, frowning, and felt a jolt in her belly as her eyes fell on the journal. She reached for it. "Celeste's diary? Is that what you came about? I was just…" She took a step toward the bed and the spirit twitched violently, her mouth coming open and a horrifying howl emerging from her thick, saggy throat.

Anna jolted to a stop, her hand still outstretched toward the bed. She felt her eyes go wide as the ghost of Rebecca Dashery disappeared into a roiling mist. The light behind Anna flickered and the bulb exploded, casting her into darkness.

She dove to the ground as the poltergeist surged toward her, only the woman's deathly face and cold eyes remaining in the swirl of violent fog that coated the surface of the table behind Anna in ice.

The woman screamed her unearthly scream again and slammed into Anna. Prickly static electricity bit her exposed skin, leaving behind a thin sheen of ice.

The ghost was gone as quickly as she came, and Anna's apartment went deathly silent.

She dropped to her butt on the icy carpet, hugging her knees against her chest and gulping air.

Her heart pounded against her ribs and her stomach twisted. She hadn't expected that. What in the world?

The journal!

Anna's head jerked up and she pushed to her feet, her hand sliding across the rumpled covers to find the leather bound diary. She heaved a sigh of relief. It was still there.

But her fingers slipped across the leather. She grimaced, yanking them away. Rummaging in her nightstand, Anna pulled out a flashlight and switched it on.

She shone it on her fingers, crying out when she saw the slimy red liquid coating them.

Blood.

Her pulse pounding in her head and her mouth dry, Anna slowly swerved the light toward the battered leather book on her bed. The silvery arc of light slipped over it, illuminating the shiny drops of bright red blood spattered across its surface.

And the telltale smears where Anna's fingers had scraped across Rebecca Dashery's horrifying message from the ether.

CHAPTER FIVE

Anna didn't sleep that night. She snapped pictures of the journal with her phone and saved them, intending to show them to Pratt and Joss in the morning. Then, wrapping brown paper around the bloody cover to preserve it, she made herself a cup of tea and turned on every light in the house. Anna finished going through the journal, determined to figure out what it was about the thing that had sent Rebecca Dashery's ghost into a supernatural tizzy.

Her eyes were bleary as the sun came up and she was none the wiser. There were a lot of stories about time spent with the governess' daughter, Wilhelmina, a.k.a. Willa Miller. Pages upon pages describing their shared pleasure in rowing the boat in the pond and trekking through the fields hunting for butterflies. As the two girls got older, Anna sensed a rift in their relationship. Celeste seemed to crave the attention of boys. Actually, at first it was one boy in particular.

Gregory Miller. Willa's brother.

Celeste's untidy scrawl filled the yellowed pages with glowing accounts of young Gregory's appeal and her friend's resistance to the idea of their growing love. As Celeste's obsession with the young man increased, her relationship with his sister degraded.

That had to have been hard for both young women.

The pages written about her love for Greg were emotionally driven, unrealistic, like you'd expect to read in a teen's diary.

Except that, by Anna's calculation, Celeste Dashery would have been in her early twenties by the time she apparently became engaged. She spoke of picket fences and happily ever afters, as if citing the plot of a Hallmark movie.

Celeste Dashery was naïve. There was no doubt in Anna's mind that the girl had been ripe for trickery and deceit. She wondered if Greg Miller had intended to marry Celeste for the Dashery fortune. By all accounts it had been sizeable back then, before Mr. Dashery died and the family slowly declined into a comfortable but hardly wealthy status.

Whoever killed poor Celeste, it seemed to Anna that all the people around her had been negligent of her feelings. Except perhaps for poor Willa. Who found herself replaced by a brother she clearly didn't trust.

Her eyes burning, Anna closed the journal and laid it carefully on the table in front of the couch. She stood up, stretching stiffly, and plodded into the kitchen to get another cup of tea. It was getting late and she had to get to the shop. But before she went to *Yesterday's Antiques*, Anna had a stop to make.

She had a suspicion why Mrs. Dashery had shown up in her home. And she wanted to make sure she was right.

~SC~

The bell on the door jangled as Anna entered *The Finishing Touch*. Milo Watson stepped through the door separating the carpet and flooring side from the funeral home side.

Wearing a canvas apron covered in stains Anna would rather not examine too closely, the town's only mortician and flooring expert looked at her with surprise.

"Oh. Hello, Miss Yesterday. How are you?"

Anna ran a finger over a display of laminate flooring that looked like wood, marveling at how realistic it appeared. She wished she had the funds to put the flooring in her store. The carpet that was currently there might possibly be older than a lot of the antiques she sold. "Morning, Milo. I'm fine. Nice rain last night."

The mortician ran pudgy fingers over his apron, his wide face flushing. "It was. Yes, it was." He ducked his head shyly. "I apologize..." He tugged the bow in the center of his gently rounded belly and pulled the apron off over his head. "I was in the basement and didn't realize I had company."

The basement. He'd been working on a body then. Suppressing a shudder, Anna shook her head. "No worries. I just stopped by to talk about the increase in my rent."

His small, dark brown eyes shifted away. "Ah. Yes. I'm terribly sorry about that." He headed toward the door at the back of the store and stopped in the open doorway, looking back at her. "Would you like some tea?"

When she hesitated he hurried to add, "It's really no trouble. I was about to make some for myself."

She smiled. "Then, yes. Thank you." She wandered around the store, adding items to her wish list as Milo puttered in the back room. Several moments later he returned with a small tray that contained two steaming white mugs and a small plate with a couple of donuts on it. "I'm afraid the donuts are just store bought. Nothing special."

"My favorite kind."

He returned her smile and seemed to relax. Milo put the tray onto a small, wrought iron bistro table and indicated one of the chairs. "Please, sit."

When she complied, he joined her, easing himself slowly into the other chair. "These old bones are getting more crotchety by the day."

Anna sipped and found the tea to be particularly good. "Mm. Thank you for this. It really hits the spot."

He narrowed his gaze on her. "You look tired."

His comment reminded her of the real reason she'd come down. Nodding, Anna set the mug down and reached to break off a chunk of a cinnamon sugar donut. "I am. I was up late reading."

"Oh? Something you'd like to recommend?" His grin widened. Sharing the same taste in literature, mostly along the horror and suspense lines, Anna and Milo often exchanged book recommendations.

"Not this time. I'm afraid I was reading Celeste Dashery's journal."

"Ah." Milo nodded as he reached for a powdered sugar donut. "I'd heard you inherited the old place. That must be exciting."

Anna noted the shrewd shift of his gaze and suddenly understood the rise in her rent. Milo was under the impression she was coming into a lot of money.

"I was…until I bumped up against Agatha Miller yesterday."

Milo's mouth twisted in a quick grimace, which he swiftly mastered. He nodded, wiping his lips with a paper napkin from the dispenser on the table. "I'd heard rumors the Millers were going to make a run at the house." He shook his head. "I just can't believe Old Mrs. Dashery would leave it to Agatha Miller."

Anna's eyes went wide. "She didn't. If their claim is real, she left it to Agatha's grandmother, their old governess slash housekeeper."

"Yes. Agatha the first, if you will. The girl was named after her grandmother."

"Oh. I didn't realize that. Well, young Agatha…"

"Martha."

Anna blinked at the interruption and he lifted a hand.

"Sorry. But that's what everyone calls her because it doesn't feel right to refer to them as Senior and Junior." Milo chuckled. "The girl's middle name is Martha." He shrugged.

"I see." Anna thought it was strange that Agatha, or Martha, hadn't introduced herself that way. "Well, she seems very convinced her grandmother has the proof of inheritance she'll need to claim Dashery Cottage."

"I'd be surprised."

When Anna turned a curious glance on him he leaned forward, wiping powdered sugar off his short, thick fingers as he fixed her with a confidential look. "Nothing personal about Agatha, I assure you. I grew up with the Millers. Agatha and I were contemporaries of a sort. I know more about them than I'd like to. Yes, Agatha worked for the family for a long time. And yes, she was as loyal as they come. But there was just something…unhealthy…I guess is a good word…about that relationship. I don't believe Old Mrs. Dashery would have left the house to them."

Anna chewed thoughtfully for a moment. Wiping her lips, she sipped her tea before asking him the question she'd been contemplating since reading Celeste's journal. "Did you know Agatha's daughter, Wilhelmina?"

Milo frowned. "I did. Tragic child."

"Why do you say that?"

He shrugged. "Just my impressions at the time. Willa was…awkward." He clamped his lips shut on whatever it was he'd been thinking about saying.

Anna's curiosity was piqued. "Does she still live in Crocker?"

"I really couldn't tell you. If she does I haven't seen her. I guess I assumed she moved away but I just don't know."

"What about her brother?"

Milo frowned. "I hope to never run across him."

The mortician's brusque response surprised Anna. "I'm sorry to pry but…why?"

Milo shook his head, pursing his lips. It was clear he didn't want to elaborate.

She decided to come at it from another direction. "Did you know he and Celeste Dashery were engaged?"

Milo blinked several times. "No." He shook his head. "That's not possible."

"It was in her journal. In fact, the engagement seems to have caused a rift between Celeste and Willa."

Milo thought about it for a moment, one finger sliding up and down the handle of his mug. Finally, he sighed. "So that's what happened."

"You knew about the trouble between Celeste and Willa?"

"Only because Willa Miller left Crocker a few months later and I only know of two times she's returned, briefly."

"She came back?"

He nodded. "When her mother took sick a while back. Three years ago, maybe. And when her brother got married."

That surprised Anna. "Greg Miller got married?"

Milo seemed to realize he'd said more than he wanted to say. He stood, gathering up his mug and the empty donut plate. "That's not my business."

Anna stood too. "Look, Milo, I don't know what Greg Miller did to you…"

The man lifted a hand to stop her. "I'm sorry, Anna, but in my business, it doesn't pay to speak ill of the people around you. Every person here in Crocker will eventually find their way onto that table in the basement. When they do, I suppose they'll die with their secrets. I won't take that right away from them."

"I understand." Anna handed him her mug. "Thank you so much for the tea and the donut. I ran out of the house this morning without having my usual fruit and yogurt."

He did a mock shudder. "Sounds to me like you ended up better off for it."

She laughed. "My taste buds would agree but I'm not sure my arteries would."

He shrugged. "You have to die from something." Then he waggled his bushy brown brows. "Sorry. Mortician humor."

She laughed. "Don't worry about the rent, Milo. I understand. To be honest, it was overdue."

"Thanks for understanding, Anna." His smile was shy as he said her name. She'd tried for years to get him not to refer to her so formally, but he treated everyone with that level of respect. As he said, pretty much everybody in Crocker was probably going to be one of his customers eventually.

She watched him amble quickly toward the small kitchen area and then remembered one of the reasons she'd wanted to stop down to see him. His acknowledgment that he knew the Millers had almost made her forget.

"Milo?"

He stopped, turning to her with an expectant lift of the bushy brows.

"I was wondering, is Rebecca Dashery by any chance in your parlor right now?"

"She is. Her viewing's tonight. I don't expect much of a turnout for it, unfortunately. She didn't have any family as you know."

Anna nodded. "I'll be here of course. Pratt will come with me."

"That would be nice, Anna. It's sad when the deceased leaves this world without anybody wishing her a proper goodbye."

Anna couldn't agree more. What she didn't want to say in front of Milo though, was that sometimes the deceased don't exactly leave this world so much as hover above it.

When that happens, they tend to dance back into it every once in a while, and cause mischief.

As Old Mrs. Dashery had done to Anna, just the night before.

CHAPTER SIX

The lights were flickering madly when Anna unlocked the door to *Yesterday's Antiques* and stepped inside. She hit the light switch and they flickered on, only to flicker back off a moment later.

She sighed. "Joss! Are you and Bess fighting again?"

The antique floor mirror that Anna kept near the dressing room in the back jiggled in its frame and flipped. The mirror was facing Anna and dead in the center was a horrifying vision of an overly made-up woman wearing a low-cut gown with ruffles rippling at the neckline.

As Anna reached back to lock the door, the brightly painted lips on the specter started to move. "That scoundrel won't let me in the store again."

Anna looked up as the chandelier in the center of the ceiling started to sway, the crystals clattering together in a soft, melodic song.

"Come down here, Joss." Anna shook her head. Sometimes she felt like a young mother dealing with a couple of cranky toddlers.

The air chilled and Joss suddenly appeared, his tall, leanly muscular form propped against the mirror. He turned a scowl on the ghost in the glass. "I warned ya g'hal. But you didn't listen."

A strident yowl filled the air and a fat, orange cat scampered out from under the wicker couch in front of the window. He stopped a few feet from Anna, turning a green-eyed glare on the mirror and offering a heartfelt hiss to the universe before hurrying over to rub his wide face over her calves.

"Good morning, Mr. Bones. How was your night?"

The big cat did a figure eight around her legs, his belly flopping from side to side as he walked, and then turned and gave the mirror another hiss.

The ghost in the glass crossed pale arms over an abundant chest and glared at the feline. "I swan, that critter's just wrathy. It's not my fault he walked through me." She shook her head. "Ain't never heard such carryin' on neither."

I gave her a look before picking up the traumatized cat. "Bess, you know he doesn't like being touched by ghosts." What Anna didn't say was that poor Mr. Bones was still traumatized from having one take a ride on him for several days once.

She didn't want to make the ghost in question feel bad about it. To his credit, Joss *did* feel bad. It was the reason he banned Bess from the store level whenever she teased the cat.

"That critter's not very game. He's skeered of everything."

"That don't mean you should send him into spasm, Bessy g'hal. I told ya 'bout that."

She rolled her heavily painted eyes and popped away, leaving a layer of ice on the surface of the mirror.

Anna kissed Bones on the head and settled him back on the floor. He took one look at Joss and hissed again, scampering through the door to the back room. Anna followed him toward the break room, where he was already crying for his breakfast.

"That beast don't need no more food, darlin'," Joss told her. "He can barely jump up on the table in the back now."

She grimaced. She knew Joss was right. Bones had been emaciated when she'd found him on the streets of Crocker. It had given her pleasure to fatten him up. But it was possible she'd gone a little too far in that direction. "I'll cut back his portions. But it won't work unless you and Pratt stop giving him snacks."

The boys liked to "drop" pieces of food for the cat all day. In Pratt's case, hunks of meat from his lunch. Joss used his supernatural energy to accidentally spill stuff onto the floor for Bones.

She hadn't had the heart to yell at them up to that point. But if Joss was going to lecture her about the cat's weight, he was going to have to help her slim him down.

As she was pouring a reduced portion of kibble into Bones' bowl, she glanced at Joss. "I got a visit from old Mrs. Dashery last night."

His brows lifted in surprise. "You don't say? Did she tell ya she give the house ta you 'stead o' that grifter woman?"

Anna settled the bowl of food down in front of a very unhappy cat and filled his water bowl. "I wish. She didn't say anything actually. It was weird. All she did was paint the journal I was reading with blood."

Joss went very still. Anna set the water bowl down and gave Bones a few scratches behind a ragged ear and then straightened, noting for the first time that her friend was uncharacteristically quiet.

She glanced his way, surprised to see him looking at her with horror writ large upon his handsome face. "What's wrong?"

"That critter did what?"

Anna frowned. "What critter?"

Joss shoved the cowboy hat back on his head as he did when he was perplexed or upset. "This ain't good, darlin'."

"What isn't…?" Then she realized what he meant. "The blood on the book, you mean? I don't think it's anything really. Mrs. Dashery's body was in the morgue two floors beneath my apartment. I'm guessing the blood came from there."

His ghostly face regained some of its usual color. "Well, that's somethin' then. I was fearful there for a moment we was dealin' with a savage spirit. It takes a lot of wrathiness to manage that type of energy."

She thought about that, wondering if Mrs. Dashery seemed that "wrathy". She was definitely agitated about something. "She seemed angry that I had the journal. Maybe Agatha Miller was right. Maybe she meant for the Millers to have the house and its furnishings after all."

"That ain't how spooks think, darlin'. The newly dead are tied to their emotions. That thing you saw weren't a rational critter." He cocked his head. "What did she look like?"

Anna shrugged. "Pretty much as she did when she was alive." She grimaced, "Except that she was covered in blood."

His dark blue gaze gained a level of intensity. "Blood? My understandin' was that she died of internal failin's. Was she bludgeoned?"

Anna frowned. She hadn't thought about it. "No. Death was ruled natural causes. Heart attack." Her gaze found Joss's worried one. "What does that mean?"

"It means the critter was tryin' ta give ya a message. There's been violence done to somebody. And the old woman wanted ya to figure out who done it."

The bell on the front shop door announced the arrival of someone. Since Anna had locked it before coming back, she knew it had to be Pratt.

He called her name a moment later.

"Back here!"

Joss' form rippled and thinned. "I reckon I best go talk to Bessy girl. Try ta smooth them ruffled feathers." He looked thrilled at the prospect.

"Good luck," Anna said, grinning. "You'll need it."

Joss disappeared as Pratt came through the door from the store. He was holding a small white bag with a big grease spot on the bottom. He stopped and looked around. "Where are they?"

Bones abandoned his empty bowl and pattered over to Pratt, his big belly swinging from side to side. Anna smiled as he rammed himself into Pratt's legs, purring so loudly she could hear him from the break room.

"What's up little man. You seem angry."

Anna laughed. "I put him on half rations. We've all made him fat."

Pratt frowned. "But I brought him this." He pulled a small can of tuna out of his pocket.

"And that's exactly why his stomach moves more than his legs when he walks," she told him with a smile.

Pratt gave her a pleading look, pointing to the desperately yowling cat trying to climb his leg to get to the can. "He knows I have it."

"Because you showed it to him!" She said with mock anger. She rolled her eyes as the combined power of both of their pleas overwhelmed her. "Okay, but just a tiny bit. He really does need to lose some weight. It isn't good for him to be this fat."

A gleam of triumph in his eye, Pratt headed for the cat's bowl. "Come on, Mr. Bones. Let's get you a treat before Nurse Ratched over there changes her mind."

"Hey!" Anna objected. She hid a smile behind her hand as she watched him open the can and dish a small amount into the cat's bowl.

Pratt put the rest of the can into the fridge as the cat wolfed it down.

Finished with his snack, Bones jumped up on a chair at the table, settling in to bathe before his nap. "So, what's up? Where's the cowboy?"

"Trying to soothe Bess' hurt feelings."

"Let me guess; she was teasing the cat again?"

"And Joss banned her from the store." Anna shook her head. "Those two."

"Yeah, those two."

She glanced over as he fought a smile. "Sometimes, I feel like the mother of three toddlers."

"Three?" He lifted his hand to very deliberately count off two fingers. "I only count two ghosts."

"And a naughty assistant," She added, walking over to wrap her arms around him. "I have my hands full."

Pratt kissed her gently and pulled away, sighing happily. "You can't fool me. You love it."

"Maybe."

He held up the bag. "I brought you a donut."

She grimaced. "I've already had my quota for the day. You can have mine."

"You ate a donut without me?"

She laughed at the hurt look on his face. "I went down to talk to Milo this morning and we had tea."

"Everything okay?"

She grimaced. "He raised my rent."

"Oh. Sorry to hear that. Are you moving?"

"No." She responded quickly before thinking about it and then hesitated. "Well, I guess I could consider it. But not necessarily because of the rent."

Pratt tucked a pod into the coffee machine and started it. "Something else happen?"

She told him about Mrs. Dashery's visit.

He looked appropriately concerned. "You'd think she'd be nicer since she left her house to you."

"You would, wouldn't you? And the way Josiah Baumgartner described her, I was kind of thinking she'd be willing to help."

"Well, to be fair, he was only talking about the issue of his bones. Mrs. Dashery might not want us messing around with her daughter's death."

"Why not? Unless she has something to hide."

He opened the coffee machine and plucked the used pod out of the well, flinging it into the trash. Carrying his mug over to the small round table against the wall, Pratt sat down and opened the bag.

Anna nearly swooned at the scent of donut wafting her way.

He pulled out her favorite, holding it up and raising his brows in question. "You sure? If you want we can go for a run later and wear it off."

The running together thing was new. They'd only started when Anna complained about gaining weight from their mutual eating habits. But their relationship had formed around the donut in the morning and the shared sandwich at lunch. She hated to give them up.

So, they'd compromised. The exercise made her feel good and it was a fun, low-stress time together that she'd grown to cherish almost as much as their breakfasts and lunches.

"Deal." She fixed herself a cup of coffee and joined him at the table, feeling her world righting itself again at the shared joy. Anna broke a chunk off the moist cheese Danish and dunked it into her steaming coffee. Before she popped it into her mouth, she fixed him with a curious gaze, "You never answered my question."

"Hmm?" Pratt swallowed a bite of glazed donut and reached for a paper napkin. "Oh. Why would Mrs. Dashery resent our meddling into her daughter's murder? She probably wouldn't. Unless she already knew who the murderer was."

Anna chewed for a moment, considering his observation. When she swallowed, she nodded. "But if she knew…" Anna stopped, a horrifying thought occurring. "What if it was her? What if she killed her own daughter?"

Pratt didn't look surprised. He'd already come to that conclusion. "It's certainly a possibility. And it would explain the bad juju you received when you touched those cards."

Frowning, Anna laid her danish down. She'd lost her appetite. "How could a mother kill her own child?"

"Boggles the mind," Pratt said. "But unfortunately it happens."

He fell into thought, his expression sad. He was most likely thinking about his last case as a police detective in St. Louis, Missouri. He hadn't told her the whole story yet. But he'd told her enough for her to know that it had been horrendous. In fact, it was a wonder he'd come out of it sane.

The same could not be said of his partner on the case.

In an attempt to help Pratt climb out of his dark thoughts, Anna made a proposition. "We need to solve the case."

He didn't seem to hear her at first, but he finally turned her way, his gaze still distant. "What case?"

"Celeste Dashery's murder. I need to know if I've inherited the estate from a murderess. Because, if I have, I'm not sure I can accept it."

He thought about it for a minute. "It's a very cold case by now, Anna."

"Yes, but it's never been solved, right?"

"No. The police came up with nothing. Everyone they considered a suspect had alibis they couldn't break." He shook his head. "I'm afraid it would be a waste of time."

"You don't have confidence in our abilities?" She peaked a brow, knowing the challenge would entice him to her point of view.

"It's not that. But I trust police work too. I doubt the investigation for a wealthy family who was well known in Crocker would have been slipshod."

"I'm sure they did all they could do, Pratt. But they didn't have access to all the resources we have."

"You mean the ghosts?"

"Yes. In fact, if we can get a little help from our ghostly friends, we might even be able to access Celeste Dashery herself."

He thought about that for a moment and then nodded. "Okay, we can give it a try. But if that...thing that accosted you at the Dashery place comes after you again, I reserve the right to reconsider."

She didn't like it. But she could understand his need to protect. She'd deal with the problem if it came to that. Because Anna had already decided she was going to solve Celeste Dashery's murder, no matter what it took.

CHAPTER SEVEN

"We need to talk to Mrs. Miller."

Anna grimaced. "I know. I've been trying not to go there."

Pratt shrugged. "Everything seems to start with the Millers. We don't know where Willa is and her brother is currently an unknown too. Mrs. Miller might not be averse to talking about her time with the Dasherys if it was a positive experience."

"What if young Agatha has poisoned her against us?"

"Then we'll deal with it." He wrapped his arm around her waist and kissed her on the temple. "I have confidence in your ability to charm her. Everybody likes you."

She blew air through her lips. "Everybody except for young Agatha Miller."

Pratt shrugged. "She's young and stupid."

Shaking her head, Anna turned the sign on the front door of *Yesterday's Antiques* to "Closed". She lifted her head as Pratt pulled his keys from his pocket. "Where's Joss?"

"From what he said I gather he was going to spend some time in the ether, trying to find Celeste Dashery."

Anna nodded. "I suppose it's possible she isn't lingering."

"It is. But I agree with you. If we can find and talk to her that will make our jobs easier. Then we'll know who killed her and all we need to do is figure out a way to prove it."

He opened the door for her and she ducked through. "That's all, huh?"

He grinned widely. "Piece of cake."

~SC~

Agatha Miller lived in a white raised ranch with unnatural looking brick along the bottom third of the façade. The yard was well kept but spare, with only a couple of small trees and two small evergreens on either side of the front door.

The neighborhood was newish, built on farmland that had once been flat and unadorned as far as the eye could see.

Despite the youth of the house, Anna noted some upkeep issues, such as a green tinge over the white siding in the front and a pile of yellowed newspapers littering the small front porch.

A tiny silver sedan, American made and probably very fuel efficient if not roomy, was parked in the short, concrete drive in front of the home's single garage.

The interior door was open when they stepped onto the porch, and an inexpensive aluminum storm door gave them a view onto the stairs inside. One short level rose to the house's main level and the other fed off a small entryway covered with cheap linoleum, descending to the lower level.

After peeking through the screen to look for movement, Pratt knocked loudly.

A long moment of silence followed.

Pratt knocked again, calling out, "Mrs. Miller? It's Pratt Davies and Anna Yesterday. Could we speak with you for a minute?"

A soft whirring sound brought their heads up and they watched as a woman who looked to be around seventy rolled into view at the top of the stairs. She was piloting one of those mobility scooters that were advertised on the radio all the time as being, "practically free!".

She was a tall woman with bony arms and legs and a gaunt face. Her tangled gray hair had an unhealthy yellow tinge to it and her hands were knobby, with prominent blue veins crisscrossing the backs. Her eyes were a cold, unwelcoming blue as she glared down at them and her lips were compressed in a thin line. "What do you want?"

Pratt tried the door and found it unlocked. He eased it open and gave the woman his patented, harmless smile. "Good evening, ma'am. How are you?"

Agatha's glare deepened. She clearly wasn't willing to let herself be charmed.

But Pratt had a lot of experience questioning resistant witnesses. He quickly read the situation and adjusted. "We had a nice visit with your granddaughter yesterday. We were wondering if you'd like to talk about the house?"

When the older woman appeared to hesitate, Anna stuck her head through the door. "Hello, Mrs. Miller. I'm Anna. I'd like to talk about your relationship with the Dasherys. It might help me understand your claim on the house better." Implied in her statement was the possibility that Anna might decide not to fight the claim. Anna didn't know if that was true, but she was willing to hear Agatha Miller's side before they went down the path of disputing it.

The woman finally motioned toward the stairs. "Come on in." Then, without another word, she backed and turned the little scooter and rolled out of view.

They found her parked in front of the window, knitting needles working manically over something formed of pink and creamy white yarn. She held it up as they approached. "Baby blanket. My son's about to have a child. It's been too long. But he got the job done. That's all that matters." Her smile pulled at the skin around her lips as if her face wasn't accustomed to the action. When her lips parted slightly, Anna nearly grimaced at the state of the teeth behind them.

If Agatha Miller had ever seen a dentist, you couldn't prove it by the gaps in her smile or the black and graying teeth that remained.

"Congratulations to you and…Greg is it?"

Pratt lowered himself onto the couch and Anna took the hard, upholstered chair in front of the room's picture window.

The woman cast a jaundiced eye in his direction. "What do you know about him?"

It seemed an overly suspicious question but, given what Anna was learning of the family, it didn't really surprise her. "I'll admit I found Celeste's diary," Anna told her. She watched Agatha's reaction carefully but didn't notice anything that could be construed as concern over the information.

In fact, Agatha shrugged. "The girl was always scratchin' away at that thing. She poured all her feelings into it. Bunch of drivel if you ask me."

"It's not unusual for young girls to keep diaries," Anna told her carefully.

Agatha shrugged again. "She didn't have many friends. I guess she was compensating."

That seemed a large thought for someone of Agatha Miller's personality. Anna realized there was more to the woman than she'd first assumed.

It wouldn't pay to underestimate her.

"I understood your daughter, Willa was her friend," Anna offered.

Agatha winced. "Wilhelmina felt sorry for her, that's all." She pointed to an ornate silver frame on the table under the window. The frame looked expensive, heavy and tarnished as only real silver does. It was out of place in a room filled with inexpensive furnishings. "There they are. They were quite the pair for a time."

The photo in the frame was yellowed, creased in the corners as if it had been carried around in somebody's pocket for a while before being tucked into the frame.

Anna leaned closer, examining the faces there. She recognized Celeste Dashery from the photos at Dashery Cottage. The girl was younger then, with her moderately attractive face filled with happy light. Her high cheekbones and slightly tilted, almond shaped eyes gave her an exotic look that her mousy brown hair disputed.

Next to her, the blocky, plain girl with the overly short hairstyle and round face looked uncomfortable in her own skin. Anna pointed to the heavyset girl. "Is this Willa?"

Agatha nodded, her eyes shining with pride. "Such a smart child. She could play chess like a pro." Her smile faded. "Wilhelmina's intelligence was wasted on the Dashery girl. All she cared about was romance and silly stuff. 'Course that wasn't going to happen for her. Not that girl."

Not a very kind thing for Celeste's old governess to say. Pratt didn't seem to like it either, judging by his next question. "Was there something wrong with Celeste? Why didn't she have friends?"

Agatha lowered her knitting and gave him her full attention. "I did care for her. She was kind and tried to overcome her natural inclinations, But the girl was strange. Always mumbling to herself. She had imaginary friends, Mr. Pratt. Lots of them."

Pratt didn't bother correcting her about his name. He merely nodded agreeably. "That was probably a little disconcerting."

"That's one word for it," Agatha responded dryly. "The girl was touched in the head. My Wilhelmina was kind to her as you'd expect. Since the two children were thrown together a lot they naturally spent time exploring and playing. But Celeste's imaginary friends made Wilhelmina uncomfortable."

"What about your son?" Pratt asked.

The woman's brows lowered over squinty eyes. "What about him?"

"Was he kind to Celeste too?"

"To be honest, he didn't have much to do with her. The girl tended to misread his actions when he was kind. She had a girlish attachment to him, which is understandable. He was…is…a very attractive and intelligent young man."

"But her feelings weren't returned?" Anna asked.

"Of course not. My Greg's always been a man who's goin' places. He has designs on a political future. That girl would have never fit into his world."

"Sometimes love doesn't care about plans and intentions."

She cast Pratt a disgusted look. "I took care of that girl since she was a baby. She was always odd. She used to talk to her imaginary creatures from her crib, waving and smiling at them when she was ten months old. That girl should have been in a place where they could have monitored her more closely. Not on my son's arm. Believe me when I tell you he wanted nothing to do with her."

"That's so sad," Anna said, frowning. "Did you talk to her mother about it?"

The woman blew a raspberry. "Rebecca Dashery didn't have a clue about that girl. She avoided her like the plague. Tell you the truth, I think she was afraid of her."

"Why would she be afraid of her own daughter?"

"The girl was unhinged. She didn't throw regular temper tantrums. She threw furniture. More than once she harmed her mother when she didn't get her way."

Anna and Pratt shared a look. That was information Anna hadn't found in the diary.

"You knew about her father, didn't you?"

Anna shook her head. "He died when she was a young woman."

"You ask me, that man was the cause of the girl's problems. He coddled her, ignored her flaws. Celeste inherited his madness and Rebecca never knew what to do about it."

"He showed the same symptoms?" Pratt asked.

"Close enough. Man spoke to ghosts. At least that's what he told me. I never saw a single ghost in that house when I was there. But he claimed the place was thick with them."

Somehow Anna didn't believe Agatha Miller was as clueless as she pretended.

Agatha shook her head, clearly disgusted. "It was just a cover for him talkin' to himself."

Anna could feel Pratt's gaze but didn't dare look at him. Clifford Dashery hadn't been crazy after all. He'd been right about the ghosts in the house. Pratt and Anna had already met one of them and Anna had experienced another. "Did Celeste ever claim to see ghosts?"

Agatha shook her head. "I wouldn't hear that nonsense. She knew better."

Pratt leaned closer, his forearms resting on his knees and his gaze earnest. "Mrs. Miller, who do you think killed Celeste Dashery?"

Her eyes went round and her fingers stopped the dip and swirl motions with the thick needles. She rested them in her lap, fixing him with a look that could only be described as disgusted. "Killed her? Nobody killed that girl. Good heavens, what in the world are you saying? Everybody knows she took her own life."

CHAPTER EIGHT

Pratt waited on hold for several minutes before his friend, Dr. Morticia Phelps finally came on the line. She sounded rushed and out of breath. "Sorry, Pratt. It's been quite a morning. I've had a breakthrough with one of my patients and I couldn't walk away from her until just this minute."

A brief silence pulsed through the line and then Pratt asked the question neither one of them wanted him to ask. "Pam?"

Morticia sighed. "No. Sorry. She's pretty much the same. I'll let you know if anything changes."

It wasn't censure...exactly...but it was as close as Morticia would come. Pratt's old partner would probably never be all right again. Her brush with evil had taken root too deeply into her psyche. But Pratt hoped the talented psychologist would one day find a way to reach the old Pam and drag her free from its influence. "I'm sorry, 'Ticia."

"Don't be. I understand. I just wish I had better news for you." She expelled a breath. "How are you? How's Anna? And most importantly, how's my boyfriend Joss?"

He could hear the smile in her voice and couldn't help smiling too. "As irritating and judgmental as ever. Joss, not Anna."

She laughed. "Guardians can be judgmental. It's part of what makes them effective. And Anna?"

"Actually, that's why I'm calling…"

"I knew it. Do I need to drive to Crocker tonight?"

"Uh-uh. I know you're busy. But I just wanted to run something past you." Along with her Doctor of Psychology, Morticia also had a Masters in Parapsychology. She'd even written a couple of books on the subject and done groundbreaking work detailing the different types of spirits. Until reading her work, and spending time with Joss and Bess, Pratt had believed there was only one kind of ghost. Scary ones.

"Talk to me. I have fifteen minutes before I need to go back."

He told her about what happened to Anna at Dashery Cottage. When he finished telling the story, there was a brief silence during which he figured Morticia was probably digesting the details. "I don't like it, Pratt."

His pulse spiked. If Morticia didn't like it, he was really worried. "Have you come across something like this before?"

"You have. Here in St. Louis."

Pratt's heart pounded against his ribs. "Please don't say that, 'Ticia."

"I'm sorry. I don't mean to scare you unnecessarily. There's a really good chance what Anna bumped up against isn't as vile and dangerous as what Pam tangled with. But the strength of its control over her…the speed and ease with which it hit her…I'll admit those things worry me, Pratt."

He scrubbed a hand over his face. "I can't let her go back into that house."

"Has she had any further experiences?"

Pratt remembered Anna's account of Rebecca Dashery's visit. "Not exactly the same. But Anna brought something home from the mansion…a diary…and that night she had a visit from the spirit of the woman who owned the house."

"Tell me exactly what happened."

He told her as carefully as he could, fighting the urge to rush through it and ask Morticia how he could protect Anna. He could almost hear Morticia sit up straighter when he told her about the blood on the journal.

"Have you tested the blood?"

"I gave it to a cop friend of ours here. He verified it was Rebecca Dashery's blood. But her corpse was two floors beneath Anna's place. In the morgue."

"Good heavens! Anna lives above a morgue? With her spectral sensitivities she should have her head examined."

"I'm going to be talking to her about that too." He frowned, staring out the window of *Yesterday's Antiques*. It had been Anna's turn to get the sandwich they'd share for lunch and she was coming back up the street. "I have to get off the phone, 'Ticia. What can I do to keep her safe?"

"Dangit! I wish I could come to Crocker."

"I'm not asking…"

"I know you're not asking. I just want to help." She thought about it for a minute. "I know someone who can help. I'll let you know when he'll be there. I'll do some research and send it along with him."

"Thanks. I'll talk to you soon." Pratt hung up, feeling better. He watched as Anna was stopped in the street by the woman who owned the flower shop up the street. The two women were smiling, chatting amiably, and Pratt's heart felt as if it might break. If anything happened to her…

"Tell me what's wrong, Puke. What trouble have you gotten Miss Anna into this time?"

Pratt turned to find Joss standing behind him, the cowboy hat twisting in his hands as proof of his alarm. "It's not good, Joss. Anna's in danger. I'm going to need your help to keep her safe."

~SC~

Anna was reaching for the door of the shop when a male voice called her name. She turned with a smile, expecting to see a customer hailing her.

She wouldn't have known who it was if she hadn't recently seen his picture in Agatha Miller's home.

He strode across the street, his handsome face fixed and cool and his hands tugging the front of a suit that probably cost as much as Anna made in a month.

He offered his hand as he stepped up onto the sidewalk. "I'm ..."

"Gregory Miller." She shook his hand. "I spoke with your mother this morning."

He inclined his dark head. "I know. That's why I'm here." He indicated the store with a jerk of his square chin. "Can we speak somewhere private?"

"Of course. Come inside." She held the door for him and glanced quickly around the store, finding Pratt standing near the counter in the back. Their eyes met for a beat and Anna widened hers in silent message. He started across the store as Joss flickered into view a few feet away.

Gregory Miller twitched as Joss appeared, his dark gaze sliding around the space as if looking for him. But he didn't focus on the spot where Joss stood, next to the mirror Bess had been whining from earlier.

"Pratt, this is Gregory Miller."

Pratt shook the other man's hand. "Mr. Miller. How are you?"

"I'll admit I've been better." He looked around, a slight twist in his lips telling Anna all she needed to know about what he thought of her business.

"You don't like antiques?"

He looked surprised at her ability to read him so closely. "I don't dislike them actually. It's just that I like clean lines and drawers and hinges that don't stick and creak."

"I understand. We all have different tastes."

He nodded. Two lines appeared between his brows. "I'm guessing you know why I'm here."

"About Dashery Cottage?"

"Yes. I'm sorry for the trouble. I understand the will mentioned you as the heir to the home and its furnishings. Frankly, I'm not sure why Mother would want to live there. That place doesn't hold good memories for her."

Joss popped up next to Gregory and shoved his face close to the other man's, his intense dark blue eyes narrowed. "This one's part of the Codfish aristocracy. I don't trust him."

Anna pressed her lips together at the strange sounding term. From years of deciphering Joss' strange colloquialisms, she knew he was naming Gregory Miller a rich businessman. He wasn't wrong.

Joss pursed his lips and blew into Miller's face.

Miller jolted backward, his gaze skimming the room. "Do you feel that breeze? It's awfully cold in here."

Pratt shoved his hands into the pockets of his jeans. "I hadn't noticed."

Anna frowned at Joss but he was grinning, clearly happy with himself. "About your mother, Gregory, I got the impression she was happy working for the Dasherys."

"Happy? Doubtful. But I'm sure there's comfort in the memories. Mrs. Dashery was a difficult woman and her daughter…" The twist in his slightly cruel lips returned. "Let's just say she could have used some help."

"Celeste Dashery was disturbed?" Pratt asked.

"To be honest, I really believe she was just lonely. Her mother didn't have much time for her and she didn't leave the house much. Her oddities made life a living hell for her at school so the old lady kept her home and had her schooled there."

"You mean her imaginary friends?"

Miller frowned. "Voices, she said. Looking back, I think the girl was schizophrenic."

That surprised Anna. "Really?"

"Your mother thinks Celeste killed herself. Do you agree?"

"I have no idea. I kept my distance from her in those days. It was just best for everyone concerned."

"Because she was in love with you?" Anna watched him carefully, expecting him to deny the suggestion. She was surprised to see a flash of something that looked like warmth flit through his dark brown gaze.

"She thought she was. But the truth is, I was just the nearest warm body. She had a vivid imagination."

"Why would she have killed herself?" Pratt asked.

He shrugged, his mask of indifference firmly in place again. "I hate to be harsh but, why *wouldn't* she have? Her entire world was in her imagination. Who knows what she might have convinced herself of. It's tragic really."

Tragic yes, Anna thought, but he'd made certain it didn't affect him adversely. Suddenly she didn't want to be around Gregory Miller anymore. He was making her stomach hurt. "You wanted to talk to me about the house?"

He looked relieved to be back to business. "Yes." Miller opened the leather folder he'd carried inside and pulled out a photocopy of a ragged, yellowed document. A single statement was scribbled across the top in an unsteady hand, the ink faded and broken on the paper. It said:

For her years of faithful service, I bequeath Dashery Cottage and all its furnishings to my housekeeper, Agatha Miller.

The missive was signed in a nearly illegible scrawl.

"That is Rebecca Dashery's signature. I've already had it authenticated."

"There's no date," Pratt noted, frowning.

"The envelope it was in had a date stamp of October 2nd, 1985."

"But that's before the will giving the house to me," Anna said. "The will supersedes this claim."

"It would if Mrs. Dashery were in a stable frame of mind. But as you know, she had dementia and was only lucid for brief periods of time over the last couple of years. We intend to prove that she couldn't have been of sound mind when she produced the will." He held the photocopy up. "Once we've proven that, this will become the determining document."

Anna's stomach sank. If Gregory Miller was half the lawyer he appeared to be, judging by his suave, unshakable confidence and expensive suit, he would no doubt do exactly that. She forced a smile. "If that's the legal finding I'll accept it, Mr. Miller."

"I'm happy to hear you'll be reasonable, Miss Yesterday."

"Of course. But I should warn you. There are things you don't know about Dashery Cottage. Things that could prove dangerous to your mother should she decide to move into it. My friends and I are equipped to deal with those things. But I'd be remiss if I didn't warn you so you'll be prepared."

Miller's face turned red. "Is that a threat, Miss Yesterday?"

Her smile might have been just a tiny bit mean. "Not from me, Mr. Miller."

CHAPTER NINE

Anna moped around the store all afternoon and then, as they were preparing to close up shop at five, decided to put the issue of the house behind her and focus on Celeste Dashery's murder. To that end, she was planning on spending the evening trying to locate Willa Miller.

But, as usual, Pratt was one step ahead of her. He'd apparently contacted their friend Bill Dresden because the uniformed cop was walking up the sidewalk toward the store. He held the small, lined paper notebook in his hand he used for taking notes.

"Bill's here," Anna called out to Pratt.

He came into the shop from the back room. "Oh good. Right on time." As Pratt joined her, Anna pulled the door open and waved at Bill.

"I thought maybe he could help us find Willa."

"You read my mind," Anna told him with a smile.

Bill accepted a brief hug from Anna and shook Pratt's hand. "I understand you two have gotten yourselves mixed up in another old murder," he said with a grin.

"Mixed up, no," Pratt responded, clapping his friend on the back. "But you know how Anna is, when things don't add up she starts asking questions."

The two men gave her a warm glance and Anna flushed. "I guess I was a cop in my previous life."

"That sounds like a mystery you should check into," Bill said with a wicked gleam in his eye.

She shook her head. "How's Glynus?"

"Beautiful and Smart. But you already knew that. The plant's keeping her too busy though. I rarely get to see her these days."

Bill's girlfriend, Glynus inherited the local printing plant, *Quality Print*, when her grandfather died.

"I'm sure things will slow down after the holidays."

Bill fixed his wide hazel gaze on Anna, nodding. "That's what she keeps telling me. But that's still six months away."

"Would you like something to drink?" Anna offered.

"No thanks. I need to get back to the station. I'm on duty tonight. But I wanted to let you know that I've found Willa Miller. She's actually living in Parkersville, in one of those new condos overlooking the river." He tore a sheet of paper out of his notebook. "I wish I had more to give you on the other…" He shook his head.

"Other?" Anna asked. "What other?"

Bill and Pratt shared a look. Bill finally asked, "Was I not supposed to tell her?"

"No. I just haven't gotten around to it. We were too busy today." Pratt settled his gaze on Anna. "I asked Bill to dig up what he could on Celeste Dashery's death. It turns out we were wrong. The police never considered it murder at all. It looks like Agatha Miller was right. Celeste Dashery killed herself."

Anna frowned. "But that's not possible, I saw…" Her words flitted away as Pratt's gaze turned dark. "I…um. I really thought I remembered something about a murder."

"Oh, you probably did. Mrs. Dashery always proclaimed her daughter was murdered." Bill waited a beat. "By a ghost."

Bill had recently been initiated the hard way into the knowledge that ghosts were real. He'd helped Pratt and

Anna on more than one occasion with a savage spirit, albeit unknowingly for much of the time. Which made the derision that was so clear on his attractive face seem strange.

Anna lifted a brow. "You don't believe that?"

"Not really. Ghosts don't hang people from ceiling beams."

Anna frowned, thinking of the high ceilings and heavy, dark beams crossing Celeste Dashery's bedroom. "She hung herself?"

"I'm afraid so. And because it was clearly a case of suicide, the officers on the scene didn't do much more than take a couple of pictures and write up their impressions of the death in their reports."

"Can we see the photos and reports?" Pratt asked his friend.

"Already sent to your email. I'm afraid you won't be able to talk to the officers, though. Beckens retired a few years ago and moved to Florida. Meeks died of a heart attack in 2004."

Pratt winced. "Okay. Well thanks for what you gave us, Bill."

His friend nodded, closing his notebook and turning back to the door. "Let's get together for dinner again soon. Glynus has mentioned a couple of times that she'd like to meet up with you guys again."

"We'll get it on the calendar," Anna said. "Thanks for your help, Bill."

"My pleasure. At least this time we're not battling enraged ghosts from the ether, huh?" His laugh followed him away down the sidewalk, a light and happy sound.

He didn't seem to notice Anna's silence or Pratt's grimace at his joke.

Anna closed the door and locked it behind their friend, turning to Pratt.

He held up the small piece of paper, giving her a grim smile. "Shall we go talk to Miss Willa?"

~SC~

Wilhelmina Miller lived in an end unit in a contemporary gray, black and white condominium building. Her unit was one of several that had a one-car garage underneath it, and Anna and Pratt had to climb a steep flight of stairs to get to her front door.

Pratt fixed a picture of young Willa in his mind and glanced around, his nose twitching at the slightly fishy scent permeating the riverside area.

When the door opened, Pratt wasn't sure he was looking at the right woman. "Wilhelmina Miller?"

The woman was tall and slender, with boy-short light brown hair that was highlighted in gold. She had a shapely mouth, a slender nose and delicate ears, the ridges of which were lined in tiny diamond stud earrings. She looked much younger than the fifty-five years Pratt knew her to be, but he could definitely see a slight resemblance to her brother Gregory.

"Yes?"

Anna smiled, offering her hand. "Hello. My name is Anna Yesterday. This is my business associate, Pratt Davies."

Willa Miller gave Anna's hand a perfunctory shake and then retracted her hand, shoving it into the oversized pocket of her loose-fitting trousers. "I've heard of you. You're the woman who's inherited the old Mausoleum."

"Dashery Cottage, yes. Though I understand your family is going to stake a claim to it." Anna's tone was light, but knowing her as well as he did, Pratt noted just the tiniest edge of bitterness in it.

"I don't have anything to do with that," Willa said. "Talk to my brother. Greg's in charge of ramrodding that through legal channels." Her shapely mouth tightened around the words. She was clearly disgusted by the prospect.

"You don't approve?" Pratt asked.

The woman shrugged. "It doesn't really matter if I approve, does it? Greg will do what he wants no matter what."

"But he's doing it for your mother, right?"

As usual, Anna's instincts were spot on. Her question shot right to the heart of it. If questioning the inheritance was really being done for Agatha, the letter in Gregory Miller's possession held some emotional weight if nothing else. If it was being done because the son wanted to ensure his own inheritance when his mother passed, the stench of his greed might be a useful bludgeon they could use to kill the suit.

"I suppose. Though mom's never seemed all that interested in it. I guess selling some of that old, scary looking furniture would help her pay some of her medical bills."

"We met your daughter at the house yesterday," Pratt said, watching Willa carefully.

She frowned, her attractive face clearly transmitting confusion. "My daughter?" She laughed. "You must be talking about Greg's kid. Martha. She's kind of a brat isn't she?"

"I'm confused," Anna said. "Your mother said Greg was going to have a new baby and that he was getting a late start. We assumed he didn't have any children."

"Martha's a bastard."

The proclamation was so coldly delivered. So cruel in the ease with which Willa Miller made it, that Pratt bristled under it. "Miss Miller, I gather you don't like your niece very much…"

Amazingly, she laughed. "You misunderstand. I love that kid. But we speak plainly in this house. No hiding behind emotional euphemisms. Martha's mother and Greg never married. She was a youthful indiscretion, nothing more. But, to his credit, Greg's done right by her. And she adores the old woman."

"Martha and your mother are close?" Anna asked.

"Like peas in a pod. Even though mom refuses to acknowledge the kid's parentage. I think she tells everybody M's mine." She shook her head. "It works out better for everyone."

Pratt wondered about that statement but held off asking. He had his suspicions and didn't want to distract her from the issue at hand. "Miss Miller…"

She threw up a slender, long-fingered hand. The nails were clean and cut short, with no polish on them. Pratt also noticed she wore no jewelry other than the studs in her ears and very little makeup. Miss Wilhelmina Miller was a natural beauty and clearly a minimalist.

"Please call me Willa."

"Wilhelmina is kind of a mouthful, isn't it?" Anna asked with a smile.

"I always hated that name. Wilhelmina is in my past. She was overweight, insecure and friendless. Kind of a sad sack. I refuse to be held back by my past."

"Very wise," Anna agreed. "You seem as though you're very happy."

"I am. I love this place. The river calms me. And I have family and friends. Life is beautiful." Presented with a slightly angry edge, her statement seemed less than sincere.

"Willa…" Pratt waited until she returned her attention to him. "What happened to Celeste in 1983?"

She blinked several times, clearly taken aback by the question. "Seriously? *Now* you people decide to investigate her murder?" Willa shook her head. "I can't believe it. You *are* a cop. I pegged you for one as soon as I laid eyes on you."

Pratt shook his head. "Not anymore. I used to be. But Anna and I are trying to find out what happened to your friend. She *was* your friend, right?"

Willa stared at him for a beat and then dropped her gaze, expelling a rush of air. "You might as well come in. This is probably going to take a while."

CHAPTER TEN

They sat on a balcony overlooking the Crocker River. With the recent rains, the river was overflowing and running fast, the sound a constant roar in the distance.

Willa Miller didn't offer them refreshments. She seemed generally unwilling to make them feel at home in her neutrally decorated, contemporary home.

The furnishings reflected its owner, lean and stylish with sharp edges and an unwelcoming aspect.

Willa motioned to two of the chairs on the balcony and then dropped into one herself. She reached for a lighter and a pack of cigarettes, lighting one quickly and drawing deep before expelling the smoke out into the atmosphere.

Pratt didn't push her to talk. It seemed impossible to do anyway. Willa Miller was tightly wound and carefully kept.

He'd seen her type before. She'd give them only what suited her and not a syllable more.

She was halfway through her cigarette before she started to talk. The words came out in a straight line, with minimal space between them. Like she was expelling them for medicinal purposes.

A verbal catharsis.

"We were drawn together because neither of us had any friends. A sad couple of outcasts, each with her own terrible secret the world wasn't capable of understanding. I accepted her imaginary friends and she accepted my..." She flicked them a quick glance. "Proclivities."

Pratt frowned. "What kind of pro..."

"That's not important," she said quickly, cutting him off. "But we were a perfect pair, Celeste and me. She was as graceful as I was cloddish and I had the intelligence to keep her interested despite her...distractions. We spent hours running the grounds and searching out the hidden corners of that old mansion. They were the happiest days of my life." She stopped talking for a moment, smoke curling from her delicate nostrils. "She broke my heart."

Pratt waited a beat to see if she would expand on that astounding admission. When she didn't, he leaned forward, fixing her with an understanding look. "You were in love with her."

Willa didn't give any indication she'd heard him, but a vein at the side of her slender throat pulsed, showing her agitation.

"What happened?"

"My brother happened. He watched her fall for him, laughing behind her back, and then threw her away like a used tissue. I couldn't stand to witness her pain. It was too horrifying. I had to stop it." She shook her head, a single tear sliding down her cheek as she stamped the cigarette out in an overflowing ashtray on the table.

"How did you stop it?" Pratt asked quietly.

Her jaw flexed, her lips compressing. She stared into the rushing gray water as if it held the secrets of a lifetime.

Maybe for her they did.

She'd hidden herself away for decades, never admitting what she was for fear she'd be rejected for it. To Willa Miller, the constantly running water probably represented freedom and strength and independence. Everything she didn't think she had.

He was surprised such an intelligent woman would let herself be cowed like that.

"Did you kill her, Willa?"

Her head snapped around. Her eyes narrowed and her hands clenched around the pack of cigarettes she'd been holding, crushing it. "I could never have killed her. I loved her."

"Then who did? Who killed Celeste Dashery?"

She let her gaze return to the soothing madness of the river. "*He* killed her. Gregory. Because she was going to ruin the perfect plan he had for himself."

"Can you prove that?" Anna asked gently.

Willa blinked as if she'd forgotten Anna was there.

Pratt doubted that. Willa Miller didn't miss much.

"No. I just know he did it. He was so angry when she told him she wanted to marry him. She tried to pressure him, telling everyone they were engaged and then threatening to get mother fired when he denied it." Willa sighed. "She should have known better but she was desperate. Greg couldn't be threatened. He lifted his fist to her, told her she wasn't going to ruin his life. He crushed her like a bug under his heel. He's a monster."

"Your mother believes Celeste took her own life," Anna said. "From what you're telling me it sounds plausible."

"She wouldn't have done that."

"Sometimes people do things we don't expect," Pratt offered gently.

Willa shook her head, another cigarette suddenly between her long fingers. She lit it and sucked smoke into her lungs before responding. "No. She trusted me to fix things. And after a while, she moved on to the next hapless male victim." Her lip quivered.

"She asked you to intervene with your brother?"

"Yes. I tried everything. I even told him Celeste would be rich someday. He loves money. That actually almost convinced him. But in the end, he said he couldn't saddle himself with a mad woman."

"Because she heard voices?" Anna asked.

Willa turned almost angrily to Anna. "Voices? I see you've talked to Gregory. He never understood how special Celeste was. He could never see her gift for what it was."

"What was it?" Pratt asked.

Willa pulled long and hard on the cigarette and sent the smoke curling out over the river below. "It was spectacular and rare." She finally turned back and met his gaze. "She spoke to the dead. Spirits. Ghosts. And they spoke to her." Willa leaned closer, the cigarette in her hand glowing softly in the dying evening light. "And something didn't like it when she was killed. Something in that terrible house didn't like it at all."

"Did anyone else see the ghosts?" Anna asked.

Willa frowned. "I believe her father did. Before he died, he used to take Celeste on walks through the hallways of the big house." She glanced toward Anna. "You've been there? In the house?"

"We have." Anna smiled. "I can verify that Celeste was probably really connecting to something there."

Her eyes widened slightly. "You felt them too?"

"Anna did more than that. The thing…whatever is so angry…did something to her. I thought for a minute I'd lost her."

Willa stubbed the cigarette out, reaching for a glass of iced tea that no longer held any ice. Judging by the sizeable ring on the glass tabletop and the overflowing ashtray, Willa Miller had spent some time out there before they'd arrived. "Yes. My mother used to tell me about it. After Celeste was gone, the thing was known to throw things around. It damaged a bunch of that old furniture. The only room it didn't rampage through was her bedroom." Willa shook her head. "Mom retired after that. She was terrified to be in the house."

"And Mrs. Dashery? Was she scared too?"

Willa reached for the cigarette pack and seemed to change her mind. She picked up her tea instead, her fingers going white as she gripped it. "Amazingly not. Mom described walking into the library once and finding the old woman standing there, chin up, eyes staring straight ahead, while books and chairs and pictures flew around her. It was like she was standing in the eye of a hurricane. Nothing touched her."

Anna and Pratt shared a look. That had to be significant. Though he had no idea how.

Anna frowned. "How did Mr. Dashery die?"

Willa finally gave in and lit another cigarette. "He had a bad fall in the Library. He was on the ladder, trying to grab an old, hardbound book when the ladder slid out from under him. He hit his head on something and it killed him instantly."

The library again. That seemed to be the center of everything. "Was there anyone else in the house who could have killed Celeste?" Pratt asked. "Any friends or neighbors whom you noticed acting strange?"

"There was a young pastor in town. For a while I thought he and Celeste might have been having a fling. He came to see her almost every day for several months and then just stopped. I heard them arguing the day before he stopped coming and asked Celeste about it. She denied the fight, said Pastor Fredrick just considered her a project. That he was trying to get her and the old woman back to church. They'd stopped going after the old man's death."

"But you didn't believe her?" Anna asked.

"I'm not sure. He'd certainly seemed like he could be into her. But I'm afraid my brother's treatment had turned her cynical and I doubt she returned the interest." Willa shook her head. "Too bad. I'm sure he would have been a much better choice for poor Celeste." Her lips twisted bitterly and Pratt wondered if it still pained her to talk about the possibility of the woman she'd loved marrying a man.

Willa glanced at her watch. "I'm sorry. That's all the time I can give you today. I have a friend coming over."

They said their goodbyes and saw themselves back through the house. Willa Miller sat in the chair with her back to them as they left, smoke curling from the cigarette between her long fingers.

An attractive blonde woman opened the door as Pratt was reaching for it and exclaimed in surprise. "Oh. You startled me."

"Sorry about that."

The woman looked around, her blue gaze showing disappointment as they started past her, out the door. "She's on the balcony," Pratt told the visitor, earning himself a grateful smile.

Anna stopped short as they started down the steps to Pratt's truck. "We should have asked her which church."

"No need. I know the church where Pastor Frederick ministers. It also happens to be the one where I go."

CHAPTER ELEVEN

Aside from her surprise at hearing that Pratt went to church at all, Anna was shocked to learn he was a Lutheran.

"You know, I'm Catholic. I'm not sure we can see each other anymore."

He chuckled. "Why not. The two religions are remarkably similar."

"Yes, but Lutherans only pass the offering plate once per service. That borders on heresy."

His laughter was much heartier the second time. "Well, mostly we're just Catholics with fewer rules. I think we can work something out."

"Good! Then you'll become a Catholic?"

"Not a chance. If it makes you feel any better I'll whip myself on Fridays if I eat meat."

She sighed expansively. "That might work. But there's still the offering plate issue."

"I'll work on a fix for that. Maybe I can bring a plate to church and pass it around to the Church Ladies begging for them to fill it with powdered sugar donut minis and hard cookies."

She laughed just as Pratt opened the front door to Trinity Lutheran Church.

The laugh echoed through the entry and danced through the open doors into the nave.

The man who'd been standing behind the podium at the front of the long, wide room looked up with a ready smile at the sound. He stepped down and hurried down the red carpeting of the center aisle toward them. When he saw Pratt, he offered a hand. "Mr. Davies. How are you?"

Pratt let his hand be enclosed in Pastor Fredrick's large hands. "I'm fine, Pastor. How about you? Are you feeling better?"

"On the mend, Lord willing." He turned to Anna and reached for her hand, enclosing it as he'd done with Pratt's. His hands were warm and soft, callous free. But then the Lord's work was of the spirit and the mind rather than the muscles. "How are you, Miss Yesterday."

Anna must have looked surprised that he knew her because he grinned widely. "You don't remember me."

"I…I'm so sorry."

He chuckled, patting the top of her hand before releasing it. "We met at the Apple Blossom Festival, last Fall. You were hovering possessively over young Mr. Johnson's apple cake as I recall. I was afraid to take a piece for fear you'd stab me with your plastic fork."

Heat infused Anna's cheeks as she laughed. "Guilty as charged. Pierce's cake is to die for. I swear I gain five pounds every year. I almost hope he doesn't bring it this year so I won't make myself sick over it again."

The pastor's brown eyes sparkled with good humor. "Gluttony is a sin, my dear. I'd advise praying on it and, I'm sure Father Regis would prescribe ten or so Hail Mary's for the transgression."

Anna shook her head. "You're terrible."

"Not at all," he said with a wide grin. "I'm just trying to make sure I get some of that cake this year."

"All right, you've shamed me. I'll just collect my one, or five, pieces and go hide in my apartment to snarf them down in guilty privacy."

The pastor laughed heartily. "Now, as much fun as this has been, I have a sermon to prepare so…" He cocked his head, the short brown hair touched at the sides by a liberal wash of gray, and turned serious. "What can I help you young people with?"

"We wanted to ask you some questions about Celeste Dashery."

Fredrick frowned. "Oh my. I haven't heard that name for a while. Such a sad end for such a lovely girl."

Anna couldn't help thinking that everyone they talked to had a different version of Celeste.

"We understand you and she were close?"

"As a pastor and congregate, yes. I spent some time ministering to her in the hopes I could get her and her mother to return to Trinity. I felt the Lord might help them through their troubles."

"Troubles?" Pratt asked.

"Why yes. Poor Mr. Dashery's death. I'm afraid both mother and daughter took it very hard. They stopped going out into the world. Closed themselves up in that big house. It wasn't healthy."

"How was Celeste's state of mind when you spoke with her?"

Pastor Fredrick arched a gray-brown brow at Pratt. "Other than sad? I'd have to say she was a bit…fidgety is probably the best word. She seemed nervous. I found that strange but put it down to concern about their future. I happen to know the family was having some money troubles when her father was alive. His death didn't alleviate it much. Though I do understand there was a small insurance settlement."

"It was judged an accident?" Pratt asked. "His death?"

"Yes, I believe so." Fredrick's face showed surprise. "Do you think otherwise?"

"No. It's just that, well when insurance is awarded…"

"You can't possibly believe one of those two women killed him?"

Pratt shrugged. "People are capable of a lot of things. For example, we spoke to Celeste's old governess."

"Agatha Miller." Pastor Fredrick nodded. "She used to come to Trinity before she became infirm. Now I visit her occasionally."

"Yes. She believed Celeste killed herself. If she had something to do with her father's death, it would make sense she'd be nervous and possibly suicidal. Do you know if she saw anyone? A therapist or anything?"

"Actually, I did suggest someone." He held his head for a moment, appearing to be digging for a name. "I'm sorry, it was so long ago. I think I still have the name on file. Can I call you later with it?"

"That would be very helpful." Pratt said.

"Pastor, did Celeste mention a romance with Gregory Miller?" Anna asked.

"She didn't give me a name, but she did tell me there was a man. I sensed she was struggling with a big decision and counseled her to take care. Her heart and her nerves were in a fragile state."

"What did she say?"

"It didn't make sense. But then I learned soon enough that a lot of what the girl said didn't make sense. I'm afraid she was a bit off."

"What did she say that you found odd?" Pratt said, nudging the pastor gently.

"That it was too late. The decision was already out of her hands." He shook his head. "I didn't know what she meant and she wouldn't elaborate." He sighed. "I'm afraid I didn't do the girl much good."

"What about Willa Miller?" Pratt asked.

"Willa was a good friend. But I sensed tension between them as well."

"So if you were determined to help, why'd you stop going to Dashery Cottage?"

The pastor looked down at his feet, clearly uncomfortable. He shook his head. "I shouldn't have. I know that now. But Mrs. Dashery was most insistent."

"She told you not to come to see her daughter?"

"She did more than tell me, son. I'm afraid she very clearly threatened me."

"Threatened? How?"

The pastor finally lifted his tortured brown gaze. "She'd...learned...some things that I'd done that I wasn't proud of. It wasn't as bad as it seemed but I was young and new in Crocker and I was certain if people found out...well...I didn't want to lose my position in this wonderful church. I was weak. And when I learned of Celeste's death I realized I might have saved her. I might have kept her from doing..." His eyes filled with tears. Pastor Frederick sniffed loudly. "I'm sorry. I really need to get back to my sermon."

He turned away and strode quickly back down the aisle without giving them another look.

CHAPTER TWELVE

Anna's phone rang when they were climbing back into Pratt's truck. She looked at the ID and was shocked to see it was from Yesterday's Antiques. She quickly answered it.

"Hello?"

Static met her greeting and Anna's pulse spiked. "Hello? Joss? Is this you? What's wrong?"

Pratt caught her look of fear and slammed the truck into gear, tearing backward out of his parking slot and accelerating toward town.

"Joss, talk to me." Her favorite ghost had only called her one other time that she could remember. And it had been because there was a crisis. Anna knew it took an immense amount of energy for her friend to send his voice down a phone line. Energy Joss couldn't spare if he was dealing with a catastrophe. "We're coming, Joss. Just hold on, okay?"

More static, then, "…darlin'…"

There was a strident scream, the sound of a raging wind and something crashing to bits near the phone. Anna put the phone on speaker and turned a worried gaze to Pratt.

He paled. Slamming his foot down on the gas pedal, he sheered right on two wheels and sped down Main street, past

The Finishing Touch and the small gravel lot where Anna parked her car.

The oversized windows of Yesterday's Antiques flashed light and shadows into the quickly darkening streets. As they watched in horror, the glass of one window burst outward and a man flew through the air, slamming to the street right in front of the truck.

"Pratt!" Anna screamed, bracing herself on the dashboard as horror swept through her in a breath-stealing wave.

Pratt slammed on the brakes, the big tires squealing and the back end shimmying sideways as it jerked to a stop.

No thumps. No bumps that would indicate they'd run over the man who'd been expelled from her store.

After a moment of stunned silence, Anna grappled with the door handle and launched herself out. Pratt beat her to the bleeding man and was checking his bloody throat for a pulse as Anna dropped to a crouch beside him.

"Is he...?"

"He's alive. Pulse is strong. I don't expect he'll stay out for long." Pratt looked at the man strangely and Anna wondered fleetingly if he knew him, but she wasn't going to find out right at that moment.

A terrifying howl rose up from inside the shop and Anna ducked as a hundred-year-old dining room chair flew through the breach in the glass, smashing into the street a foot away from them.

Anna straightened, desperately searching the darkened inside of the store for her friends. She couldn't see anything through the darkness. "Joss!"

The whirlwind spun past the window, a low-level growl emanating from its depths. It slowed at the sound of her voice, and Joss' disembodied face emerged from the chaos, wearing a murderous expression. "Stay out!" he boomed, his voice smacking against the surrounding buildings and reverberating down the street.

She started forward, torn about what to do. Her instincts were yelling at her to help her friend. But in all things spiritual, Joss generally had the upper hand.

Generally.

Anna had been known to use less violent weapons successfully against the denizens of the ether. Weapons such as intelligence and kindness.

Neither, however, would be of much use against the mindless rage of a savage spirit.

Pratt's hand settled on her arm. "Don't even think about it. He's got this."

She shook her head, her stomach twisting into knots. Her gaze skimmed the spot on the street where the man had been and she cast a questioning gaze toward Pratt.

"I put him in the truck. He should be safe there from flying debris."

She nodded.

The chandelier in the shop flared brightly and Anna's horrified gaze cataloged the chaos in her store. Furniture flew in circles around the space, broken glass spun in smaller whirlwinds everywhere. Her beloved antique cash machine bobbled violently in the air.

Paintings were torn to bits. Antique clothing was shredded. And something orchestrated the destruction from the space directly below the light.

The air there was thick, swirling with manic agitation. Any debris which approached the spinning column was flung away in a violent arc. The shadows clung inexplicably to a spot in the center of it all. And ice sparkled on everything within five feet of the savage spirit.

Anna wished she could see a face.

"Leave us be!" screamed Joss in a disembodied voice. The dancing cash machine suddenly flew across the room, hitting the column of spectral air and shattering it into bits of frost that sprayed through the air and disintegrated.

The machine crashed to the floor, embedding itself in the elderly carpet.

Of course! It was made of cast iron! It would temporarily disperse spirits. But the fix wasn't permanent.

Silence pulsed along the street. A car door slammed behind them and they turned to find the man from the street limping toward them. He was wiping blood away from what looked like a dozen cuts on his face and neck.

The man was older than she'd expected, probably in his late fifties or early sixties. He had a ruddy face and a thick cap of dark hair that was peppered with strands of silver. Despite the slight limp, the man moved like a cop, and the gaze he cast over the suddenly quiet store was a cop's gaze.

Pratt moved forward, offering his hand before pulling the man into a hug. "Officer Bowler. It's nice to see you again."

The name seemed familiar. Anna thought he might have been someone from Pratt's past in St. Louis. "Are you all right?"

The man gave her a grin that showed bloody teeth. "What this? This is nothing. I've had worse."

She shook her head.

Officer Bowler nodded toward the silent store. The chandelier had stayed on and they could easily see the mess that had been left behind. "It looks like your guardian finally got rid of her."

Anna frowned. "How did you…?"

"I'm guessing Morticia told him." Pratt grinned at his friend. "Am I right?"

"Yeah. She told you I was coming, right?"

"Well, she told me she was sending someone to help. I didn't realize you two were working together."

The older cop nodded. "After you left…" He frowned, slowly shaking his head. "I guess I never really was able to put that whole thing behind me. I no longer had any interest in being a cop. It seemed so much less important than helping people deal with things like that." He pointed to Anna's destroyed store.

She stared at the mess, tears filling her eyes as the reality of it started to sink in. She'd be financially ruined.

The two men's voices droned on behind her. She didn't hear a word they said. She'd gone numb from shock.

Pratt's arm dropped around her shoulders. "We'll make it right, honey."

She shook her head, sniffling. "It's all gone."

Bowler stepped up beside her, crossing his beefy arms across his chest. "I know that's bad, Miss Yesterday. But I'm afraid it's nothing compared to the real problem."

Anna wrapped her arms around herself and shuddered. She wasn't sure she could face the news he seemed about to give her.

"What do you mean, Bowler?"

"That…thing in there is more powerful than anything else I've encountered. And Morty and I have come up against some doozies over the last year. If it wasn't for your guardian there…" He pointed toward Joss, who'd rematerialized, looking decidedly transparent and wobbly. "I'd be dead for sure and there'd be nothing left of your store at all."

To Anna's view there was nothing left anyway. But she shoved all that aside. Joss needed her help. He'd saved her again. Probably cost himself dearly using so much energy trying to warn her on the phone. And he looked like he was about to topple over.

"He needs me."

But even as she started to step forward, the air inside the shop began to thicken again. And in the blink of an eye, everything within the four walls of the shop was covered in a glistening, perfect layer of ice.

It would have been beautiful if it hadn't been so terrifying.

Anna's gaze met Joss' across the distance and she saw the fear there. She started to run. She hit the doorway and slipped on the ice, skidding sideways and slamming into the remains of an old farm table. Pain radiated up her side but she scrambled to stand anyway.

She was dimly aware of a roaring sound building across the store. Winds wept past, blowing her hair into her eyes and pelting her with broken pieces of glass and torn paper. She ducked, shielding her face with her arms as Pratt covered her with his body.

A low, drawn-out keening sound rose within the wind, accompanied by the graveyard stench of a savage spirit.

Pratt grabbed her under the arms. "We need to get out of here."

"I can't. I have to help Joss."

"You can't help him. You'll only get in the way."

Anna shook her head as a soft, terrified mewl came to her through the bedlam. Her head snapped up and she spotted Bones, cowering beneath a massive cabinet. "Bones! We have to help him."

Pratt patted her shoulder. "You get out of here. I'll get him."

Anna nodded, her gaze drawn to the thickening air across the room. It was bigger than last time. The mass that was forming appeared to be ten feet tall and as wide as her arm span. A woman's shape was forming within its midst.

Eyes, the color of a fall forest blinked open, and a face as pale as snow appeared with the eyes. Long, light brown hair blew as if in a hurricane around the round face, and the angry slash of a mouth split open.

Suddenly a hand appeared, a slim finger jabbing in her direction. "You took it!"

Anna shoved to her feet, unable to move any further out of sheer terror. She shook her head.

"I didn't take anything."

The figure blipped and reappeared several feet closer.

A hissing sound emerged from under the cabinet and Pratt swore as Bones no doubt scratched or bit him. The poor cat was probably beside itself with fear.

Anna knew just how it felt.

The spirit flashed again and it was suddenly five feet away, close enough to turn Anna's skin to ice and lock her breath in lungs that no longer seemed to work.

"You took it!" the disembodied voice screamed over the din. The wind in the store turned rabid, digging at Anna's skin like claws and whipping her hair and clothing violently around her. Chunks of broken furniture pelted her, nails sticking out to slash at her skin.

A figure plunged through the door and the spirit whipped around. With an ear-splitting shriek of rage, it charged the ex-cop.

Officer Bowler didn't even blink. He lifted the shotgun he was holding and fired it into the spirit. She jerked once and then gathered herself, charging again.

Bowler shot her once more and she dissipated into mist.

Almost immediately the room started to warm. The ice melted within seconds, leaving everything it had touched soaked with water.

Anna stumbled backward, hitting the wall beside the door and leaning against it panting. She shoved the tangled mass of her hair off her face and looked around.

Pratt was sprawled half under the cabinet, a still squalling Bones writhing and growling in his arms. His face and forearms were covered in bleeding scratches and his handsome face was folded into a scowl. "Damn cat."

Anna's lips twisted in an attempt to hold back her smile. "You can let him go now."

Pratt had barely loosened his grip before the big cat shot out of his arms and hightailed it to the back room, where Anna had no doubt he'd find the tightest, darkest hidey hole he could and stay there until he got too hungry to hide anymore.

Anna didn't blame him.

Pratt pushed to his feet. "Is everybody okay?"

Anna nodded, glancing toward Bowler. "Thanks Officer Bowler."

Bowler shook his head. "Just Bowler if you don't mind. The officer thing is in my taillights."

Pratt nodded toward the gun. "That's pretty cool. What is it?"

"Simple concept really. Lead shot and salt pellets. Works like a charm."

Pratt grinned. "Your invention?"

"Among other things." Bowler shared the smile. "I like to tinker."

"Thank goodness for that," Anna breathed.

"How long will it keep her away?" Pratt asked.

Bowler shook his head, frowning. "Usually a good day or so. But I've never had to put two barrels into one before. That's one pissed off specter."

"'Savagerous', as Joss would say," Anna agreed.

The chandelier above their heads flickered and went dark with a popping noise. They all went very still. Anna's pulse shot up and she wanted to curse. "Please tell me that can't be her again."

"I wish I could," Bowler growled. He cocked the shotgun barrel and slid two more cartridges into it.

The light flickered back on and a small ghost, garishly made up and dressed in a tawdry dress with a hem that brushed her knees in front and fell to the floor in a flounce behind, eased into sight.

Anna let go of the breath she'd been holding, her tension diminishing.

Until Bowler raised his gun again.

"No!" Anna jumped toward him, slamming her hand against the long barrel. "That's a friend."

Bowler lowered the gun. "Sorry."

"No worries," Pratt told him, slapping him on the shoulder. "You're allowed to be a little jumpy at this point."

Bowler chuckled.

Bess stood beneath the light, wringing her hands. "Jossy's in a bad way."

Anna's heart twisted painfully. "Can you help him?"

The saloon girl shook her head, her glossy blonde sausage curls bouncing with the movement. "He's absquatulated back inta the ether. It's the only way. But he wanted me ta tell ya. That wrathy g'hal wants the journal you took." Bessy's colorful face folded into a judgmental scowl. "This was all your doin'."

CHAPTER THIRTEEN

A Crocker City Police cruiser slid silently up to the curb, lights flashing, as Anna and the men were trying to figure out how to secure the store for the night.

Bill Dresden climbed out of the cruiser and stood in the street, door still open, a shocked look on his face. "What in the world happened here?"

Pratt and Bowler hefted a huge piece of plywood and held it while Anna pounded nails to anchor it to the window frame. "You don't want to know," Pratt told his friend. "What are you doing here? Just cruising through?"

"Not hardly. I got a noise disturbance call."

Anna handed the hammer to Bowler and he finished securing his side. Rubbing her hands on her jeans, she walked outside and started picking up debris. "Who complained? This place is like a ghost town after dark."

"A guy named Miller." Bill shrugged. "Says he was driving by and there was all sorts of commotion here."

Anna and Pratt shared a look. "Gregory Miller?"

Bill nodded. "That's the guy." He frowned. "You know him?"

"Sort of." Pratt went inside to grab a large trash can and carried it out to the sidewalk. He and Anna threw pieces of glass and wood into it as Bill watched. "He's trying to steal the Dashery house out from under Anna."

Bill's expression turned shocked. "He's one of *those* Millers? Dang!"

"Yep," Pratt said, flinging the arm of a chair into the trash can. "Pretty big coincidence he called this in, don't ya think?"

"Yeah, I do think. Maybe I need to look into Mr. Greg Miller. See if there's anything worth knowing about him."

"That would be very helpful, Bill. Thanks," Anna said, giving him a tired smile.

Bill nodded. "All that aside, I doubt Mr. Miller brought this ghost to wreck your place."

Pratt and Anna straightened, sharing a look.

Bill chuckled. "You didn't think I'd recognize the signs? Come on, you two. Stop trying to protect me and let me help."

Pratt pulled his work gloves off and handed them to Bill. "Okay, you can start right now. We're going to be here all night if we don't get some help."

Bill glanced at his watch. "I'm just about off duty anyway. Tell you what, I'll swing home and change and be back in a few minutes."

"Sounds good. Thanks."

Bill touched Anna on the arm. "We'll make this right, Anna."

She forced a smile onto her face. "I know."

But she really *didn't* know. She'd lost almost her entire inventory because of that ghost. She could only assume it had been Celeste Dashery's spirit since she apparently was looking for the journal. Anna was glad the diary was in the safe in her office or it would have probably been ripped to shreds in the haunting.

As Bill left, Anna turned to Pratt. "Why do you think she wants that journal? It's not like she can write in it anymore."

He shrugged. "You've been all the way through it?"

Anna nodded. "There was nothing there which seemed important. Certainly nothing that gave me a hint as to who killed her."

"Well, I'd say, judging from tonight's experience, there's something important in those pages. We'll just need to figure it out."

Bowler came outside with his arms full of debris. Pratt looked at him and stilled, his face flushing.

"What is it?" Bowler asked.

Pratt glanced back at Anna. "Bowler just ticked something in my brain. He's working with Morticia…"

Anna shook her head, not understanding.

"The therapist," Pratt said. He shook his head. "I can't believe I didn't see it."

"See what?" Then her eyes went round as she realized what he was thinking. "Ah."

"Was there anything about her therapy sessions in the journal?"

"No. Nothing at all. That's strange isn't it?"

"I'd say so. Celeste Dashery liked to write down mundane things that were important to her. I can't believe she'd never mention the therapy sessions."

"There has to be another journal," she said.

"Yep. I guess we're going back to Dashery Cottage after all."

~SC~

They'd worked most of the night cleaning up *Yesterday's Antiques*. Pratt was alarmed at the extent of the damage. He and Anna's friends had been doing their best to prop Anna up, but there was sadness in her gaze that morning which Pratt would have done almost anything to remove.

Still, the only way through the current mess was forward. And the first step, if they were going to figure out who killed Celeste Dashery and help her ghost be put to rest, was to find out about her therapy sessions.

Pastor Fredrick had emailed the name of the person Celeste had spoken to when she was alive. Pratt had called Morticia early that morning to see if she knew the woman. And to thank her for sending Bowler their way.

"I do know her," Morticia assured him. "She's a competent therapist."

Something in her tone set off alarm bells. "Competent? Not good?"

"In this case, no," Morticia said, sighing. "I'm afraid Beverly Addams has her small, wide feet firmly planted in the physical world."

"She doesn't believe in spirits?" Pratt shared a look with Anna, who grimaced. "Not the best therapist for a young woman who reportedly spoke to them."

"Understated but true. I think that, if the subject of spectral activity had come up, Doctor Addams would have made that poor woman feel as if she was ready for a padded room. I attended a conference with Bev once and I remember she was a bit of a snob and not the most flexible person in the world."

"Better and better." Pratt shook his head. "I'm starting to feel really sorry for Celeste Dashery."

"Yes, Me too. Has Mr. Bowler been helpful?"

"Eminently. The guy's fearless."

Her laugh was musical. "He is, isn't he? He's been a godsend for my work."

"Anna and I really appreciate your sending him. He probably saved her store last night. That was one ticked off ghost."

"So I heard. Mr. Bowler called me late last night. If you need me there…"

"No. You have your hands full. I think we'll be fine. But thank you for the offer."

"Okay, but if that changes just call. I'm sorry I didn't have time to do that research I promised, but I'll try to get to it tonight."

"No worries. I know you're busy.

Pratt disconnected a moment later and pulled up to a white brick building that looked like it had once been someone's home. The sign in the yard held Doctor Addams' name in flowery letters and gave a website underneath her designatory letters.

He glanced at Anna, biting back the urge to ask her again if she was okay. She wasn't okay and he knew she wouldn't be for a while. Not until they got the current mess behind them.

"You ready?"

She nodded and climbed out.

Walking around the car, Pratt joined Anna on the sidewalk. They stood staring at the small, unassuming building. A curtain twitched behind the picture window on the left. Pratt wondered if Doctor Beverly Addams lived in the home where she had her practice. Judging by the gardening gloves and digging tools on the ground next to the flower bed, he suspected she did.

He rang the bell and the door was opened immediately. A tiny woman who was nearly as round as she was tall stood looking at them, her small eyes blinking from behind very thick glasses. Her gray hair was upswept in an old-fashioned style that reminded Pratt of Aunt Bee from Mayberry RFD. The woman wore a suit that might have come from the Mayberry days too, with a ruffle-necked blouse beneath the cranberry colored jacket and a skirt that ended well below her wide knees. "You must be Pratt Davies?" The doctor shook Pratt's hand, ignoring Anna almost completely in the exchange.

"This is Anna Yesterday, my colleague."

Addams skimmed a disinterested gaze toward Anna and then stepped back. "Come in. I can only give you a few minutes. I have a client coming at the top of the hour."

Pratt nodded. "This won't take long."

They followed the therapist into a living room that was straight out of time, complete with lamps bearing tasseled shades and doilies on the tables. A knick-knack shelf on the longest wall held an array of porcelain collectibles that Pratt figured probably took an hour to dust.

Doctor Addams indicated a pair of matching upholstered chairs across from an unwelcoming flowered couch. They sat down in the chairs as she took the couch. A still steaming cup of tea sat on the long table between the furniture. Addams took a sip from it and settled it back to its saucer with a gentle clink of porcelain on porcelain.

She didn't offer them anything.

The chair Pratt was sitting in was harder than a board, with a back so upright it was impossible to get comfortable. But it was pristine like the rest of the house.

"You wanted to ask me about Celeste Dashery?"

"She lived in the home I inherited," Anna said. "Dashery Cottage? We were wondering if you had any case notes you could share with us. Or are you aware if she was keeping a journal of your visits together?"

Beverly Addams sniffed. "I only saw her a few times and I have no idea if she wrote about our visits. As far as my case notes, I wouldn't have much and I won't share them with you. But I can tell you the gist of what they contain. I was unable to help her, I'm afraid. The family didn't accept my findings."

"What were your findings?" Pratt asked.

"Celeste Dashery was a troubled young woman. She was schizophrenic and delusional. I encouraged the family to commit her."

"You believed she was dangerous?" Pratt asked, surprised.

"I did. Generally, when a patient hears voices I'm prone to taking drastic measures."

"Why's that?" Anna asked.

Beverly glanced her way, her wrinkled lips puckering. "Isn't that obvious? It's never very long before the voices tell them to kill someone. In this case it's a blessing the girl only harmed herself."

Anna and Pratt shared a look of surprise.

"Surely you don't mean that?" Anna said angrily.

The therapist's small, bulbous nose lifted with arrogance. "I know it sounds harsh. But I'm an expert in my field, Miss Yesterday. I know what I'm talking about. Schizophrenics can be very dangerous."

"Did Celeste show that tendency?"

"Not specifically, no. But I knew where she was headed. There were indications."

"What indications?"

A young black woman wearing a pretty summer dress walked in and glanced at them, inclining her head in greeting. She lifted a cup of something to her lips and then moved around the couch and sat on the opposite end from Doctor Addams. She crossed her long legs and took another sip, then fixed her brown gaze on them and let her lips curve into a smile.

Seemingly unaware, Beverly Addams gave Pratt an assessing look. She apparently decided he was worthy of her thoughts because, with another sniff, she told him. "She believed she was speaking to ghosts. That young woman was very disturbed. The occult is an evil practice and those who indulge in it are generally evil too."

Anna glanced at the young woman on the opposite end of the couch. In response, she raised slender black brows and sipped again from her cup. Anna shook her head. "Just because she spoke to spirits doesn't mean she dabbled in the occult."

Beverly's arrogant gaze narrowed. "I wouldn't expect you to understand, you being a shop owner and all…"

The woman said "shop owner" as if Anna made a living scooping poop off the streets.

"Those who are obsessed by the paranormal are sick and demented individuals. They are living in a fantasy world of dark and corrupt thoughts. Add that to the schizophrenia and you have a mass murderer in the making."

"I'm sorry, but I couldn't agree less. I happen to be one of those people who speaks to spirits." She glanced toward the other woman on the couch and smiled. "I occasionally prefer their company to people who sit in judgment of others and think they know everything." She stood up, inclining her head toward the young black woman. "Have a nice day."

"You too, hon," the woman replied in a husky voice.

Beverly frowned toward the other end of the couch. "What game are you playing at?"

Pratt stood too. He smiled at the tea drinker and turned to Beverly. "You know, if you'd open your mind a little, you might find room in there to acknowledge the young woman sitting next to you. She seems very nice. I'm sure you'd hate her."

"What young woman? Have you lost your mind?"

He followed Anna out of the house and they stopped on the sidewalk outside, turning toward the picture window. Through an opening in the draperies they could see Beverly Addams staring hard at the other end of the couch, a perplexed look on her fleshy face.

Pratt hooked an arm through Anna's and they started toward the car. By the time they climbed inside, they were both laughing so hard they were in tears.

CHAPTER FOURTEEN

Dashery Cottage smelled musty when they entered. Anna looked around the entryway, her palms moist with dread. She'd have felt infinitely better if Joss were there with them. That thought brought another one that was even more worrisome. It had been almost a full day since the attack at *Yesterday's* and there was still no sign of her favorite cowboy.

He'd never willingly left her alone for so long. Although, she guessed extreme weakness wasn't a willing condition.

What was even more concerning was the fact that Bess hadn't been able to find him either. Anna could tell by the way the saloon girl had been moping around the store all day as they swept and repaired what they could, that Bess was worried about Joss too.

"He'll be fine."

Anna turned to Pratt, amazed as always by his ability to figure out what she was thinking. "I'm trying to keep the positive thought."

Pratt nodded.

"About time you kept your promise."

Anna jumped an inch off the floor, her heart pounding against her ribs. Her gaze snapped to the large cabinet by the wall, which Josiah Baumgartner was lounging against. He had one arm resting on the heavy furniture and his legs crossed casually at the ankles. "You promised to find my bones."

Pratt locked the door behind him. "We've been busy."

The ghost's face folded into a frown. "What could possibly be more important than your commitments here?"

"Believe it or not, Baumgartner, your misplaced bones are the least of our concerns."

The ghost wavered and blipped. He was suddenly standing a couple of feet away. Anna gasped and he looked at her strangely. "I mean you no harm, Miss."

She frowned. "After one of the resident ghosts here destroyed my business and threatened my friends, you'll forgive me for not believing that."

"You don't say? Which spirit was it?"

"Celeste Dashery," Pratt told him angrily. "You wouldn't know anything about that, would you? You led us to understand she was unavailable."

Baumgartner slipped his hands into the pockets of his trousers and frowned. His handlebar mustache twitched. "Strange. I assure you, I've not spoken to the girl. But then she and I were never all that close. I'm not surprised she's avoiding me."

Anna blinked, realizing how stupid they'd been. "You knew her when she was alive."

The spirit looked at the floor, seemingly unwilling to respond.

"Baumgartner," Pratt warned. "If you want our help you'll need to help us first."

The ghost expelled a sigh that frosted the air. "It is true. The girl and I were *compadres* in her day. She liked to converse about the silliness that was her life and I was willing to listen. It gets dashed boring haunting a house for hundreds of years."

"She grew up with you."

He inclined his head.

"Then you should know who killed her and why."

Baumgartner's dark gaze turned icy. "Alas, I was in the ether at the moment when she died. My first awareness that she'd joined me in the great beyond was when she showed up there."

"Convenient," Pratt said darkly.

Josiah shrugged. "Perhaps it seems that way to you. But I can assure you it's not all that unprecedented. The ether calms and strengthens us. We go there in times of stress..." He stopped suddenly, seemingly realizing he'd said too much.

"Something stressed you around the time of her death?" Anna asked.

Baumgartner went very still and his gaze skipped away, evasive. His form wavered and Anna thought he was going to disappear, but he held himself together and finally nodded. "That womanizing hoister was here. He made Celeste cry and I lost my temper."

A feeling of dread made Anna's nerves flutter. "What man?"

Josiah shook his head. "The devil's name is inconsequential. He was evil and cruel. He and Celeste walked in the garden and then Celeste took to her bed in a fit of tears."

Gregory Miller, Anna thought. "What did you do?"

Josiah didn't look at Pratt. He seemed strangely unhappy with whatever he'd done. "The mongrel deserved it."

"*What* did he deserve?" Anna asked.

"It was a simple thing really. A fireplace poker alongside the head. And he never made Miss Celeste cry again."

She couldn't believe her ears. "You attacked Gregory Miller?"

The spirit blipped, his head coming up and his mustaches twitching. "Why no. Why would I harm the Miller boy? It was the other one I killed."

"Other one?"

Baumgartner expelled another blustery draft. "That oversexed fiend who seduced her and then dumped her for another. He's the villain I felled. And I'm not apologizing for it."

"You killed someone? Here in Dashery Cottage?"

"Are you a simpleton?" Baumgartner asked Pratt. "That's what I've been saying."

"But how?" Anna glanced at Pratt. "Surely we'd have heard something."

"There are ways to keep things from being known. I was in the ether at the time, but I heard them talking later. The old woman had him dragged out of here and buried in the garden. Very neatly done, if I might say so."

"You don't know who buried him?" Pratt asked the ghost.

Josiah shook his head.

"How did Celeste take it?" Anna asked, frowning.

"Not overly well, I'm afraid. She expelled me from her sight. That is why I was hiding in the ether when she died. And the true reason I don't have an inkling about the villain who killed her."

"Where did they bury the body?" Pratt asked, his handsome face dark with intensity.

"Beneath the gazebo by the pond."

Pratt pulled out his cell. "I'll call Bill."

She nodded. As Pratt walked away, already explaining to Bill that they needed to dig up a possible body in the garden, Anna turned to Josiah.

"Do you know if Celeste kept a second journal? One where she might have written notes about her visits with the therapist?"

Josiah frowned. "Therapist? I have no idea who that might be. However, she did keep a diary. I believe you've already located it."

"Yes. I was hoping there was another one somewhere."

He lifted his hands. "I apologize, Miss. I cannot help you with that."

Anna nodded, rubbing a hand over her eyes.

"You appear drawn. Are you ill?"

"No. Just tired. Your buddy Celeste really did a number on my store. We've spent most of the last twenty-four hours cleaning it up." When he didn't say anything, Anna looked up to find him staring at her. "You don't by any chance know why she attacked us, do you?"

"Why yes, I do."

She blinked, surprised. "You do?"

He cocked his head, his eyes narrowing. "You surely aren't as simple as you appear."

Anna gritted her teeth. "Just answer the question."

He shrugged. "You removed her journal from Dashery Cottage. She's never been away from home before. I'm sure it's quite disconcerting for her."

Anna had a face-palm moment. "The journal is her anchoring object?"

He lifted his brows. "I have no idea to what you are referring. But I do know that nothing in life was quite so important to Celeste as that journal."

Anna sighed. "I'll bring it back right away."

"That would be wise."

She dropped wearily into a chair. "That little mistake probably cost me my store."

Baumgartner lowered himself elegantly into another chair, crossing his long legs at the knees. "Don't despair, Miss, there are plenty of treasures here to make you whole again."

"If only it were that easy. I'm afraid the Millers are trying to take it away from me."

His head came up, his mustaches twitching. "You don't say?"

"I do." Anna laid her head back and closed her eyes. Then she had a thought. Opening her eyes again, she looked at Josiah. "So Mr. Baumgartner, how did you come to be stranded here at Dashery Cottage?"

He tugged his cravat and shook his head. "Alas, it was poor luck of the worst sort. All of the Dashery gentlemen have been over-fond of gambling you see. Zachariah

Dashery was no different. He held thrice-weekly card games right there in that library. I was a regular."

She nodded. "Go on."

He pursed his lips, making the mustaches dance. "I'm afraid Zachariah didn't take to being cheated at cards in his own library. Turns out the man was rather a good shot with a Gentleman's Boot Pistol."

"He shot you?"

"Unfortunately, he did."

The front door opened and Pratt came back inside. He looked at Anna. "No record of a murder here at that time. As far as we can tell, it never happened."

"I assure you it did," Josiah said snottily, while examining his nails.

"It would help if you could tell us the boy's name," Pratt told the spirit.

"Oh, did I neglect that? My apologies. Easterman. I couldn't guess at his given name. But his people were well known in this area at the time. I believe he was visiting his kinfolk just up the road."

~SC~

Anna stood back from Pratt and Bill as they carefully dug and sifted through the moist, black earth beneath the gazebo. The structure itself had been as carefully as possible broken into pieces and set aside, its deliberate destruction causing Anna to skim a sad glance its way every few minutes or so.

Or maybe it was the dried clump of flowers resting on one of its benches that was drawing her interest.

There's been some discussion about waiting until they could get a team that was trained and experienced in the retrieval of remains. But that team would have had to come from the Medical Examiner's staff in Nashville, Indiana and a tentative request from Bill told them they wouldn't make it to Crocker for at least a day or two.

Anna and Pratt didn't want to wait. If there was another body on the property...a potential savage spirit to cause future problems for whoever inherited the house...they wanted to find it and put things to rights.

Besides, Pratt thought practically, it was an important piece of the mystery of Celeste Dashery's death.

Bill was carefully wielding a shovel as Pratt sifted through the dirt with a three-pronged hoe. They'd found the tools in a garden shed that butted up against the high brick wall which surrounded the garden area.

They'd spread a clean canvas tarp over the ground next to the excavation site and had been placing objects they uncovered from the dig that might be connected in some way. So far they'd dug up a plain black button, an ancient pipe with a clump of gluey ash still inside the bowl, and a tiny hand-knitted sock that looked like it might have belonged to a doll.

They'd gone nearly six feet into the earth, far enough to hit a harder, more clay-like dirt that was much more difficult to dig carefully through.

Bill rubbed his sleeve across his sweaty face. "You're going to have to use the hoe through this. I'm afraid I'm going to cut through something with this shovel. This stuff's harder than a rock."

Pratt jumped down into the hole as Bill hoisted himself out, dropping down to sit on the edge. "I'm starting to think we're on a wild goose chase here. It seems unlikely, with the gazebo to cover the grave, that servants or whoever Mrs. Dashery assigned the task to would dig so far down and into clay. It's tough going."

"The gazebo might have been added later. It looks ancient but it's been over thirty years since this would have happened. Plus, they would have been motivated to make sure he was never found," Bill offered.

"There is that."

"Don't forget," a soft voice said behind Pratt. He looked over his shoulder to where Anna crouched at the edge. "Willa Miller was a big, strong girl. I suspect her mother was a big woman too." She shrugged. "Unless they dragged Greg into the mess."

Pratt nodded. "You're right. If Mrs. Dashery was looking for discreet help to hide a body, the Millers would be the obvious choice. I'm just getting…" The metal tips of his hoe scraped across something that sounded like rock. He scratched carefully across it again and the tines snagged on something. "Bill."

Their friend jumped back into the hole as Pratt held the hoe steady, taking care not to pull on it for fear he'd destroy important evidence.

Bill slid his fingers down the tines and around the item snagged on the tip. He carefully slipped the tine free. "Okay, you can pull it out now."

Pratt handed the hoe to Anna and moved to the side so he could see what Bill was doing.

The cop held the item between two fingers and scraped dirt away with the other hand. "It feels like fabric."

When it was clear, Pratt could see something that looked like draperies. "What is it?"

Bill carefully dug around the fabric, uncovering more of it until his careful excavation uncovered the starkly white hue of bone. "I've got a hand." Bill jerked his head toward the end of the hole. "The head should be about there. Can you loosen the dirt for me?"

An hour later they had an entire body uncovered; its aged skeleton covered loosely in clothing that could easily have been from the early nineteen eighties. The body had been wrapped in drapes and wore men's jeans, darkened and half rotted in spots with time and moisture, and a button-down shirt with oversized points on the collar. "Looks like its male," Bill said. "At least the clothes are men's."

Pratt nodded. "We need to get this to the ME in Nashville and find out how he died."

Bill climbed out of the hole and pulled out his cell. He walked away from them as he reported the body and requested transport for it to Nashville, Indiana.

Pratt stood in the hole, staring down at the remains of what was probably Celeste Dashery's boyfriend.

"Quite a twist in the story, isn't it?" Anna asked softly.

He glanced up. "Yeah. I guess we can scratch Easterman off the list of possible murderers."

"Unless Baumgartner's timing was off. Ghosts sometimes lose track of time and history. Easterman could have been killed after Celeste."

He nodded. "Good point. We'll have to lock that down."

"I guess there's nothing more we can do here today," Anna said.

"No. I guess not. Unless you want to look for that journal?"

"Maybe later. We owe Baumgartner a search for his bones too. Turns out his information was right."

"Yeah. It looks that way." Pratt's head snapped up. "I could use something cold to drink. And maybe a sandwich."

She slipped her arm through his and they headed for the garden gate. Pratt called out to Bill and waved as Anna pulled the door open. Their friend waved back and continued talking on his phone. He had a lot of work ahead of him in retrieval, reporting, and getting the necessary testing done to determine who the bones belonged to.

Pratt didn't envy him that work. "I wonder if the Eastermans still live on this street."

She shrugged. "I'll research that when we get back to the store."

The garden gate was in a secluded section of the side yard of the big home. Tall evergreens and unkempt fruit trees lined the moss-covered flagstones that formed the walkway. The stench of rotted apples competed with the sweet smell of lilac from a large bush near the gate.

Birds sang and chirped, fluttering happily from one tree to the next and feasting on the worms infesting the rotted fruit.

Anna sighed, resting her head on Pratt's shoulder. "This place sure has a lot of sadness tied to it."

He started to respond and stopped, catching movement out of the corner of one eye. "Wait here," he told Anna as he started running.

The flash of white he'd seen just ahead, at the bend in the walkway flanked by a row of tall, narrow evergreens, ducked out of sight again as he turned the corner. He stepped up the pace, speeding through the overgrown maze of mature greenery to the spot where an ancient fountain trickled a weak stream of water into a leaf-filled basin.

As he emerged from the walkway maze into the relatively open area of the fountain, something shot out of the shrubs and hit him at the ankles, sending him sprawling toward a concrete bench.

With a surprised cry, Pratt saw the bench coming up to meet him and managed to shove one hand out in time to divert himself from the worst of the impact.

Despite his efforts, his head slammed into a corner of the unforgiving surface and the world went black in a shock of instant pain.

CHAPTER FIFTEEN

"Pratt!" He was crumpled at the base of a stained concrete bench, blood running down a cut on his temple.

So much blood.

She crouched down beside him, her eyes filling with tears. "Pratt, oh no, oh no. Wake up, please." She gently patted his cheek and checked the pulse in his throat. He was alive. And a moment later he twitched, his eyes blinking open on a groan.

When he tried to sit up, she stopped him. "Just lie there a moment. I'll call Bill."

He shook his head and then grimaced. "He's getting away."

She stopped with her phone in her hand. "Who's getting away?"

Pratt pushed upright, leaning against the bench with a groan. His face was gray and there were tiny lines of pain around his eyes. "Whoever tripped me. I saw something ahead of us on the path and tried to catch up, but he was too fast. And when I came out by the fountain something smacked my leg. I went down and hit my head."

"Did you get a look at him?"

"No."

Anna dialed Bill and, a moment later he came running up the path. "Are you okay?"

"He'll be lucky if he doesn't have a concussion," Anna said, frowning. "He said someone tripped him."

"Can you describe him?"

Pratt shook his head. "But I smelled…" He frowned. "It sounds strange, but I smelled flowers."

Bill glanced toward the front of the big house. "Stay here. Let me go see if I can find him."

Bill ran off in the direction of the street and Pratt stood up. "I guess we can rule out a ghost for this."

Anna nodded. "I've never known one to skulk around in the bushes. But I guess there's a first time for everything." She gave him a strained smile. Between finding the body in the garden and Pratt being attacked, Dashery Cottage's allure was definitely fading.

Bill returned with a broken clump of fresh flowers in his hand. "I found these in the street. I think somebody might have run over them." He held them up and they did a slow dip toward the ground. "Maybe two somebodies."

"I guess I didn't imagine the smell of flowers. Do they have a tag on them? Maybe we can find out who bought them If we can figure out where they were purchased."

"'Fraid not. Why would somebody be coming here with a bunch of flowers?" Bill asked.

"The Grave."

Both men looked at Anna.

"Didn't you notice the dried clump of roses on the bench of the gazebo? It looks like somebody knew that body was there."

"Somebody who still mourns it," Pratt added. He looked at Anna. "I think we need to find out if the Eastermans still live in the area."

~SC~

"According to Bill, Wynetta Delf is Henry Easterman's Aunt. She lived four houses down from Dashery Cottage and across the street. Henry stayed with her from the time his parents were killed in a hunting accident in Africa in 1973." Anna glanced over at the building as Pratt parked his truck. "Nice place."

He nodded. "It looks like Mrs. Delf has money." Pratt helped her down from the truck and took her hand. "Apparently her mind is fairly clear so hopefully she can tell us about the days surrounding Henry's death."

Anna frowned. "Did she even know he was dead? Because, if she did, that means she was complicit in it somehow."

"According to what Bill was able to dig up, she never filed a missing person's report. It's one of the things I wanted to ask her about."

"It's so sad to think he's been lying in that hole all these years and nobody knew or seemed to miss him."

"Somebody missed him," Pratt said, his fingers twitching with the need to rub the throbbing spot on his head. They'd stopped into the emergency room just long enough to have it checked out and bandaged, but his head was killing him.

She grimaced. "How's your headache?"

"Just about what you'd expect from crashing head first into concrete."

She squeezed his hand.

Pratt pulled the outer doors open and Anna preceded him into an area that was tastefully done up in soft neutrals, with furniture that exhibited clean, elegant lines. An attractive woman who looked to be in her early forties sat behind a French Country style desk with a computer monitor on its tidy surface. She was typing away on a keyboard when the bell jangled softly and she looked up, smiling widely. "Good morning. Are you here to visit one of our guests?"

Guests? Pratt noted with some amusement. As if they were on vacation at a hotel. He supposed to some it might feel like a vacation. From what he'd learned about the place since hearing that Wynetta Delf was there, it was really a pretty sweet deal for someone who needed a little extra help and care. "Yes. We'd like to see Wynetta Delf. I called about an hour ago."

"Yes." The woman stood up, smoothing a well-fitting butter yellow suit and coming around the desk to offer them her hand. "I'm Natalie."

"Pratt Davies. This is my associate Anna Yesterday."

Natalie shook each of their hands. "It's a pleasure to meet you. I'm so glad you checked in earlier. Normally Wynetta would be in the Afternoon Pick-Me-Up class, but since you were coming she elected to remain in her rooms. I'd be happy to escort you?"

"That won't be necessary. If you'll just tell us what room?"

"Of course. Wynetta is in 303." Natalie said without checking her computer. Clearly, she'd done her homework before they'd arrived. Pratt doubted she knew the room numbers of each of the over three hundred residents at the *Dazzling Sunset Residence Home.* "The elevator's just down the hall there. Third floor, of course." She beamed at them and watched as they headed in the direction she'd indicated. They passed a dining room that still had a few stragglers chatting over coffee or tea and, on the right, a room with several elderly people dozing in chairs. On the door was a sign announcing the Afternoon Pick-Me-Up. Pratt chuckled. "I don't think it's working."

Anna snorted out a laugh.

An elderly man with a walker called out as they stepped into the elevator. Pratt held the door for him as he made amazingly good time down the hall. "Thank you, young man."

"My pleasure," Pratt responded.

The man moved to the back of the oversized elevator and lowered himself to a padded bench along the wall, groaning. "Getting old stinks," he told Anna with a gleam in his eye. "But it's way better than the alternative."

Anna chuckled politely. "This is a beautiful place to live."

113

He nodded. "I like the breakfasts. They give us a good meal at dinner too. But take my advice and don't eat supper here." He made a face not unlike a two-year-old confronted with a plate full of broccoli.

The door dinged open on three and the man struggled to his feet. Anna reached to help. "No, no, young lady. I can do it. Only exercise I get all day." He preceded them out into the hallway. "You visitin' somebody on this floor, are ya?"

"Wynetta Delf," Anna told him pleasantly. "Do you know her?"

The man nodded and started off down the hall. Pratt and Anna followed. "Happens she lives right next to me. Nice gal." He turned to them and waggled a pair of bushy eyebrows that reminded Pratt of caterpillars. "Bit of a hottie too."

Anna flushed in surprise but then she laughed. "Well, she's lucky to have such a wonderful neighbor then."

"Yes, ma'am, she is." His faded brown gaze sparkled with good humor. He slipped a plastic key into the lock of number 302. "It was nice chatting with you folks."

Anna and Pratt exchanged a look, grinning. He knocked on Wynetta's door and it drifted open under his knuckles. Pratt automatically reached for the weapon he no longer carried. "Hello?"

"Come in, come in."

Pushing the door open all the way, Pratt found the owner of the chipper voice sitting on a short couch beneath a large window with a paperback in her lap. She was a tiny thing, probably no taller than four feet ten, and wore a soft pink sweater set and white cotton slacks. Her stark white hair was styled softly around her face and there was a perfect circle of pink on each crepey cheek.

She closed her book and removed her reading glasses as they stepped into the room. "Come on in. Don't be shy." Wynetta flapped a hand, indicating that Anna should come over to see her. "My, my, such a pretty thing. Sit, sit. Would you like some tea?"

"No thank you," Anna said "We just had lunch." She lowered herself into a black and chrome leather chair across from Wynetta.

Wynetta grimaced. "We call it dinner here. And it's terrible. I much prefer the suppers."

"We'd heard something like that. Mrs. Delf," Anna said, looking like she was fighting a smile. "I'm Anna Yesterday. This is my friend Pratt Davies. We wanted to ask you a couple of questions about your nephew."

"Henry? What's that boy done now?" She asked as if they were discussing a naughty toddler. "He always was one to get into trouble. Just like his parents." She shook her head. "Why my sister was in Africa in the first place is beyond me."

Pratt took a chair next to Anna. "She was killed there?"

Wynetta nodded. "Along with that husband of hers. It was his idea to go to Africa. I know for a fact my sister would never have left Henry behind if it was up to her."

"Did Henry take their deaths hard?" Anna asked.

"Of course he did! He was only fifteen at the time. A difficult age as it was. And then to suddenly lose both a mother and a father…" She shook her head. "Tragic."

"When was the last time you saw your nephew?" Pratt asked.

She scrunched up her face thoughtfully. "I believe it was when Mr. Mosley died just after my forty-fifth birthday so that's…what? Thirty-five years ago?" She blinked as if just realizing how long that was. "My goodness. It's been a while, hasn't it?"

"Mr. Mosely?" Pratt asked. He wondered if there was another player on the Chessboard he'd need to take a look at.

"My cat. He was such a sweet boy. But he suffered terribly from the cancer." She shook her head.

"Ah." Pratt and Anna exchanged a look. Her eyes had a suspicious sparkle in them. "Were you worried about Henry just disappearing like that?"

"Oh no," she blew a raspberry. "He was always talking about seeing the world, that one. I expected he'd gone off to do just that."

"Did he say goodbye?" Anna asked softly.

Wynetta's expression turned sad. "He didn't. I'll admit that surprised me a little…"

And hurt her too, Pratt would wager.

"But he and I didn't always get along. In fact, we had kind of a big row the day before he left."

"What was it about?" Pratt asked.

"Who can remember that far back? I recollect something about a girl. But I couldn't tell you the details. Young Henry fancied himself something of a lothario." A nostalgic gleam filled her gaze. "He was a good-looking fella. Like his dad. I didn't care much for Henry's daddy but I could always see what Wendy saw in him."

"Wendy was your sister?" Anna asked, smiling.

"Yes. Pretty girl. Sweet and amenable. I'm afraid she was ripe for the plucking." Wynetta shook her head, glancing around. "Wendy would like it here."

Her tone was so wistful it tugged at Pratt's heartstrings. He couldn't imagine what it was doing to Anna. She had a much softer heart than he did. Years of being a cop in St. Louis had made him cynical. "I'm sorry she can't be with you."

She nodded, her gaze narrowing on him as if seeing him clearly for the first time. "Are you all right, son? What happened to your head?"

Pratt smiled away her concern. "Just a little accident. It's nothing."

"Well that's good." She seemed to forget his head and switched directions in the blink of an eye. "Did you find Henry? I wouldn't mind seeing him again."

Anna leaned forward, clasping her hand. "I'm afraid not. But if we do, I'll be sure to tell him you want to see him. Deal?"

The old woman nodded. "That's very sweet of you, honey. Are you sure you wouldn't like some tea?"

"Actually," Pratt said. "I'd love some. Should we go down to the dining room?"

"Oh no, dear. I have everything we need right here. Even have some of those windmill cookies. You ever had those. They're pretty good for store-bought."

CHAPTER SIXTEEN

"I'm pretty sure we can rule Wynetta out as the person who put the flowers on the gazebo," Anna said.

"And she certainly didn't knock me down in the garden," Pratt said. "I guess we're back where we started."

"Maybe we should find out where Greg Miller's been today," Anna suggested.

Pratt gave her a slow smile. "That sounds like an excellent idea, boss." His phone rang and Pratt looked at the ID. "It's Bowler. Hey, Bowler, I hope you're not calling to tell us there's been another incident at the store?"

"There has, but it's not the kind you're referring to. We have a visitor of the flesh and blood kind."

"Who is it?"

"He wouldn't say. Just kept yelling at me to get you down here to talk to him. He's really snotty and he's dressed like a lawyer."

"Ah. Speak of the devil," Pratt gave Anna a look. "We'll be there in five minutes."

~SC~

In his capacity as *Watcher of the Shop*, Bowler had made himself useful directing repairs to the front window. When they walked into the store, Anna was pleased to see him replacing some of the trim on one of her display cabinets that had been damaged in the savage spirit attack.

What she was less pleased about was the tall, elegant form of her currently least favorite lawyer standing nearby, scowling.

Miller descended on them with righteous indignation as soon as he saw them. "How dare you!"

Pratt moved smoothly in front of Anna and lifted his hands, palms out. "Mr. Miller, I'd advise you to take a step back and a deep breath. Whatever you came to speak to us about, you're going to do it calmly and reasonably or you'll be leaving."

Miller lifted a perfectly manicured finger and poked it in the direction of Pratt's chest. "How dare you accost my sister. Hasn't she been through enough already?"

Anna slipped out from behind Pratt. "First of all, Mr. Miller, we didn't accost anybody. We asked her a couple of questions which she seemed happy to answer." Anna narrowed her gaze on him. "What exactly has your sister been through? She seemed safe and healthy to me."

Miller turned a hostile gaze on Anna, his mouth tightening into a grim line. "She's not well."

"I'm very sorry to hear that," Pratt said. "What's ailing her?"

"Willa's personal problems aren't any of your business…"

"Except that you made them our business," Anna interrupted. "Since you're accusing us of being insensitive toward her. So, what exactly is wrong with your sister?"

Miller jammed his hands on his hips and looked at the ground as if fighting for control.

"I don't know about your sister's physical condition," Pratt said softly. "And you're right, that wouldn't be any of my business. But I can tell you it's been a while since I ran up against someone as unhappy as she is." Pratt crossed his arms over his chest, tilting his head as he went on. "At first I thought that she's been trying to hide the fact she's gay for so long, she feels uncomfortable owning up to it now. But in this day and age, being gay isn't even shocking. It's become accepted, even welcomed to much of the population. So, I have to ask myself...and you, apparently...why is Willa so unhappy? What happened to her that she's having trouble getting over? Did it have something to do with Celeste Dashery's death?"

Miller's dark head shot up. "You've got a lot of nerve accusing my sister of murder..."

"I never accused her of murder. At least not of Celeste's murder. Not directly anyway. I'm not at all sure that Celeste didn't die because of another murder in Dashery Cottage."

Much of Miller's belligerence fled him. Anna watched him deflate before her eyes. "You're talking like a crazy person, Davies. What other murder is there?"

"So, you're admitting that Celeste was murdered?"

The question was spoken softly, almost a whisper in the nearly silent store.

Miller whipped around to confront Bowler, who stood behind him with a hammer still clutched in one beefy fist.

"Celeste Dashery is very angry," Bowler told Miller.

Anna watched Greg Miller's face turn pale.

"Extremely angry. You saw what she did here..." Bowler swung a hand around the store. "What do you think she'd do to the people who gave her such insurmountable pain?"

Anna marveled at Bowler's intuitiveness. As far as she knew, Pratt hadn't shared with him all that they'd learned during their investigation. Yet, he'd somehow zeroed right in on the crux of it.

Miller's hands clenched at his sides. He skimmed a quick glance around as if wondering whether the ghost was still there.

"Mr. Miller, did your sister help Mrs. Dashery dispose of Henry Easterman's body?"

Miller twitched violently, his mouth coming open and his expression filled with shock. "Easterman? He's dead? When?" Quick as a snake, he grabbed the front of Pratt's shirt before anyone even realized what he was doing. "How did he die?"

Pratt reached up and grasped Miller's wrist, wrenching the other man's hand from his shirt. "We don't know how he died yet. But he was buried in the garden at Dashery Cottage."

Miller shook his head. "It's not possible. I always wondered why he left…" Miller's head jerked up as if he realized he'd said too much. "My sister had nothing to do with Easterman's death. You leave her alone." He charged out of the store, heading for a black BMW sedan parked at the curb.

"Well, that was strange," Pratt said, thoughtfully.

"Yeah. He knows about Celeste's spirit, though," Bowler told them. "He didn't even try to deny it."

"And he knew about Easterman," Anna said. The men turned to her. "He knew something about Easterman he doesn't want to tell us. And I have a feeling it might be the key to all of this."

Pratt nodded. "We need to talk to Willa Miller again."

~SC~

Willa opened the door to her elegant home before they even knocked. She looked pale and flustered, her hands continually plucking at her clothes and hair as she indicated they should come inside. "Greg was just here. He's a wreck. He accused me of all sorts of terrible things."

Pratt did a mental grimace. "I'm afraid that's my fault. I asked him if you'd had anything to do with Henry Easterman's murder."

She held his gaze for a long moment, her face chalk white, then lifted a shaking hand to her face. "I don't know what happened to Henry. He disappeared one day and never contacted me again after that." Tears shimmered in her gaze.

"We think we've found his skeleton in the garden at Dashery Cottage," Pratt told her.

Willa made a soft sound, covering her mouth with one hand. "Henry…"

"You've been carrying the secret around for decades," he said. "That must have been hard."

Willa frowned, wrapping her arms around herself. "Secret? What secret?"

"Easterman's disappearance. Surely you didn't think he'd just go away for no reason. You must have realized something happened to him."

"No. I…there were things." She shook her head. "I just figured Mrs. Dashery ran him off. She tended to do that. You know she forced Pastor Fredrick to stop seeing Celeste?"

"When?" Pratt asked. He realized she was probably trying to distract him, but allowed it with the hope of gaining more insight into what had happened.

"A few days before Celeste died." She frowned. "Sometimes I envy Celeste. She has no more pain."

After seeing what the savage spirit did to *Yesterday's Antiques*, Pratt wasn't so sure about that. "Do you believe she killed herself because she couldn't stand losing him?"

Willa frowned, "Him? The pastor?"

"No. Henry Easterman."

"I don't think…" She seemed to catch herself and sniffed again, her gaze skating away. "Maybe."

"So, you no longer believe your brother killed her?" Anna asked, reminding everyone in the room of the things Willa had told them the last time they were there. Which apparently had been all lies. The woman looked fragile, but she was apparently a very good liar.

"No. I'm sorry I told you those things. I was just angry with him. He has no right trying to steal that house away from you. Dashery Cottage shouldn't belong to us. We forfeited the right to it a long time ago."

"What do you mean by that?" Anna asked.

Willa shrugged. "My mother treated Celeste abysmally. Yes, Celeste had some mental challenges. She tended to create her own reality and cling to it with both hands. But she was kind and never hurt another soul. And Greg...I was telling the truth about him. He was a monster to her. And he used to say the most horrible things about the old lady behind her back."

"What about you?" Pratt asked.

"Me?" Willa Miller barked out an angry laugh. "I was the worst of all. I loved Celeste with all my heart. But when she took up with Henry Easterman, I got my heart broken. I'm afraid I wasn't very kind to her after that either. She had nobody. Well...nobody except the voices in her head."

Pratt would have been inclined to believe that Willa Miller had killed Easterman out of rage for having been dumped. Except there was no reason Josiah Baumgartner would have lied about killing the man himself.

"She wasn't alone, Willa. She had the ghosts. Celeste apparently spoke to them all the time. They were her friends."

Willa narrowed her gaze. "How could you possibly know that?"

"Because we've spoken to one of them ourselves," Anna told her with a smile.

Pratt's phone rang and he hit *Answer* without looking at it. "Davies."

"Pratt. It's Bill. I need you and Anna to come back here. Right away."

Pratt glanced over at Anna. "To Dashery Cottage?"

"Yeah. I've found another body."

CHAPTER SEVENTEEN

"It's probably just Baumgartner's missing bones," Anna told him as they opened the front door of Dashery Cottage.

Pratt didn't say anything. Something in the tone of Bill's voice told him it wasn't the old gambler's bones. Something tragic clung to the edges of the words Bill had spoken.

I can't explain over the phone. But it's…bad, Pratt.

Pratt felt a chill sliding down his spine. What other dark secret was the old house about to give up?

Bill was waiting next to the hole they'd dug. A man and a woman Pratt didn't recognize stood back, expressions grim. They wore coveralls bearing the Medical Examiner's logo. Apparently, the ME's office in Nashville had come through with a little help for them. Bill's head jerked up when they entered the garden and he frowned. "We found it when we removed Easterman's body." His frown deepened. "I saw a flash of white in the dirt…" His deep voice trailed off as Pratt and Anna stopped next to the makeshift grave and looked down.

Pratt thought, at first, that his eyes were playing tricks on him. It was too small to look real. "Is that…?"

"Probably only a few days old, if I had to guess," Pratt said. He scrubbed a hand over his jaw and sighed. "I guess that bootie we found didn't come from a doll after all."

Anna's hand covered her mouth and tears filled her eyes.

Pratt reached out and clasped her hand. "Buried together?"

Bill shook his head. "Doubtful. The infant was actually buried in a layer below his."

"Why?" Anna asked.

"I don't know," Bill answered gravely. "But I have a feeling that, when we find out, we'll have the answer to the mystery of Celeste Dashery's death."

~SC~

Anna and Pratt re-entered the house and Bill and the ME's people resumed excavation of the second body they'd found.

Baumgartner was waiting for them, his handsome, ghostly face looking sad. "You found the child?"

Pratt nodded. "That's what you really wanted us to find, isn't it? You weren't missing your own bones at all."

Josiah made a sound like a sigh, though his body clearly no longer needed air. "No, she did hide my bones. But I don't care. I thought if you found the child…" His voice died away and he frowned.

"You wanted its death avenged?" Anna asked, reading between the lines.

Josiah's expression turned earnest. "I don't know who killed the child. I'm hoping you'll discover the villain and get the babe some justice."

"You could have just been honest with us," Pratt said.

Josiah shook his head. "I made a vow to the girl a long time ago not to interfere. I've let her down too many times. It was important to me to keep this vow. At least the poor thing can be acknowledged at last. And the girl can rest more easily in her grave."

"Is the baby the reason she came to my store?" Anna tried again. "And why she was so angry?"

Josiah's gaze sharpened. "I told you what that was about. The journal. Celeste wants it back."

"But why?"

Josiah blipped, his form shifting away from them.

Pratt squeezed Anna's hand. "We need to take another look at the journal."

She nodded.

"If you want to know about that child, ask the old woman. She made sure the poor thing was buried deep," Josiah told them, his face a study in rage.

"Mrs. Dashery? But why?"

He shrugged shoulders that looked less substantial than they had a moment earlier. "All the old coot ever cared about was what people would think. She'd have done anything to avoid a scandal."

"Including covering up two deaths under her roof?"

"Without a single qualm," Josiah told them with an air of disgust.

~SC~

"How are we going to talk to Rebecca Dashery?" Pratt asked her. "She doesn't seem to be anchored to the house."

They exited Dashery Cottage and closed the door behind them.

"We might still be able to reach her at the morgue, a.k.a. my house," Anna said with a grimace.

"I don't like that idea," Pratt said. "Maybe Milo will let us into the basement."

"I'm sure he would."

As they headed for the driveway, they noticed a second car parked behind Pratt's truck. Anna thought she'd seen the small, light blue car before and struggled to remember where.

As they moved closer, a slender form straightened away from the car and glared in their direction. "What are you doing here?" young Agatha Martha Miller demanded in a hostile tone.

They stopped in front of her. "I could ask you the same thing," Pratt said.

The girl jerked her head toward the patrol car at the curb. "Why are the cops here?" She frowned. "You aren't going to try to keep us from taking the house, are you?"

Pratt wondered at the strange twist of rationale that had the young girl believing Anna would use the police to keep her family from a place Martha believed they legally owned. "That will be decided in the courts, I'm sure," he told her.

The frown on her pretty face didn't soften. It made her look a lot like her father. Clearly, she got the rage gene from him. Martha reached up and tucked a strand of hair behind her ear, her gaze turning speculative. "Did you find a body or something?"

Pratt's eyebrows climbed northward. "Why would you ask us that question?"

She shrugged. "I saw them roll a body bag out a while ago."

"A body bag?" Anna asked, clearly surprised.

"Sure. I watch TV. I know what one of them looks like." Her face wasn't nearly as pretty when it turned petulant. "If this is a trick to keep us from getting the house…"

Anna shook her head. "You have a completely wrong opinion of me, Martha. If your family deserves this house legally, then I'll step away from it and let you have it. I wouldn't want the home if Mrs. Dashery didn't really want me to have it."

The girl stared hard at Anna for a beat and then her frown finally smoothed away. "Really?"

Anna smiled. "Really."

"Why do you want this house so much?" Pratt asked her.

The frown reappeared. "None of your business, cop."

Pratt blinked at the vehemence in her tone. He wondered if she were mimicking a tone she'd heard from her father. "I'm not on the force. Not anymore."

She shrugged.

"Who told you I was a cop?" he asked suspiciously.

Young Martha wouldn't meet his gaze. She turned away and walked around her car, stopping with a hand on the door handle and fixing Pratt with a defiant look. "I'll answer your question because I want to. My family lived in this house for a long time. It should be ours. We have like…squatters rights to it." She skimmed a hostile glance to Anna. "That's a legal thing, you know. You never lived here so you shouldn't get it."

Simple and uncomplicated. A child's reasoning.

They watched Martha Miller climb into her ancient sports car and, amid engine clanking and overloud muffler noises, back out into the street and drive away.

"Well," Anna said. "That's one hostile teen."

"Aren't they all?" Pratt asked on a grin.

She chuckled. "Yeah. I think they pretty much are." She arched a look at him. "To the morgue?"

"Ugh! Yeah. To the morgue."

~SC~

Milo Watson led them through the door that divided the home furnishing side of his business from the mortuary side. Anna had never been on that side and, once through the door, couldn't tell it from any other funeral home she'd had the misfortune to visit.

Milo turned to them as they entered a pleasantly appointed main area. Anna glanced around, taking note of the dense, charcoal gray carpeting underfoot, the creamy white walls covered in pretty landscapes and floral themes, and the leather and wood furniture that was polished to a lemony sheen. Milo pointed to one of three solid wood doors on the far wall, each with a brass plaque on their dark wood surfaces. "She's in the Lilac Reposing Room. You'll have to be fast. Her people will be here in less than an hour for the viewing."

With a final nod, Milo headed toward a fourth door in the back and entered a room that had a large window which overlooked the main room. She watched him sit down behind a big desk and pick up the phone. His gaze rose to meet hers through the glass as he started to speak into the handset. Anna wondered if he was calling the Millers to inform them she and Pratt were there.

"Are you ready?" Pratt asked.

Anna nodded. "Let's get this over with."

The Lilac room lived up to its name in nearly every way. The walls were covered in lilac colored silk fabric and the furniture in the room, including the several rows of padded chairs awaiting mourners, displayed the same fabric. The end tables separating the small couch and upholstered chairs on the opposite end of the room held matching vases of what looked like fresh lilacs, and the flower's distinctive scent filled the room as Pratt and Anna walked through the door.

The atmosphere was hushed, thick with expectation and soft with the reality of death. It should have been a soothing place, but the unnatural presence of the corpse at the front kept it from being truly pleasant. The lighting of the room was muted, with a concentrated yet tastefully soft glow settled upon the body in the shiny, cream-colored casket across from the door.

The soft snick of a door closing behind her made Anna's pulse spike. She couldn't help remembering the last time she'd encountered Rebecca Dashery, in her room upstairs, and she wasn't looking forward to a repeat of that experience.

"How are we going to do this?" Pratt asked softly, as if afraid to wake the corpse across the room.

Anna shook her head. "I have no idea. I've never called a ghost to me before, except for Joss and Bess, and they really don't come when I call them most of the time."

Pratt's gaze slid to the coffin. "Should we maybe touch something of hers? A piece of jewelry or clothing?"

"I can try it," Anna said without enthusiasm. She approached the casket and looked down. The woman lying in the coffin looked very little like Rebecca Dashery. The color was too uniform, the lines in the elderly face too much like the lines etched into crystal tumblers. Manmade and too sharp to be real.

It was no reflection on Milo's handiwork with makeup and hair. It was more a case of the true spirit no longer being contained within the human-shaped shell he'd had to work with.

Anna had often marveled at how real her ghostly friends appeared when they were strong and solid. Every line they'd borne in real life was drawn upon their faces, every tiny flaw or spark of uniqueness remained in the image fed by their spirits.

She'd come to recognize that individual spirit as the thing which made a person real. Not the blood and air keeping the shell alive.

Anna reached out and touched her fingertip to the simple cross hanging from Rebecca's wrinkled throat. The metal felt warm beneath her touch. Ironic given the fact that its wearer would never offer warmth again.

"Mrs. Dashery? I'd like to speak to you. Will you come to me?"

Anna felt silly asking the question into an empty room. Pratt's presence at her back didn't help. As the moments lengthened and nothing happened, his silent existence made her feel foolish and inept.

She decided to give it another try. Closing her eyes and trying to focus her mind, Anna opened her senses to the unseen, reaching for the ether as she'd never dared to do before.

For a long moment there was nothing.

But slowly Anna became aware of the cold. It was a moist cold that started in her core and seemed to spread outward, until her teeth clacked together with its invasive force. She lost herself in the haze appearing before her inner vision. It was a swirling mist, sparking under a distant gleam of light that was too diffuse to isolate and name.

Shapes moved in the mist, unformed and constantly shifting. She felt a thousand hostile gazes there, every one of them concentrated on her.

The fog was disorienting.

Her mind began to lose its focus. Her memory started to fail.

Yet an urgency remained. She knew there'd been a reason she'd sought the ether. Even if she couldn't remember what it was.

Her thoughts felt frozen like the mist, and her body had disappeared, leaving her without a form to move.

Suddenly, the shapes in the mist seemed to converge and move in her direction, only their eyes recognizable in the haze.

Hundreds of gazes, filled with hostility and mistrust, moved inexorably closer, roiling the mist with their movements.

Anna made a sound of fear, but it was only in her mind. She had no lips to speak and no feet to move away. She was disembodied, frozen into inaction, and she could feel the anger at her presence, pulsing through the brittle fog and twisting within her frozen heart.

She fought to pull a cogent thought to the forefront of her mind. Why had she come to the mist? She had to know or she could never leave. There'd been a purpose, if only she could remember...

A familiar form surged forward out of the mist, causing Anna to yelp with surprise and fear. The sound was only in her mind, and the form standing before her was only half visible...a dark, amorphous shape with piercing, angry eyes. *You shouldn't have done it...Celeste.*

Anna longed to scream a denial. To run away. But nothing was as it should be. She was trapped inside death, hovering on the edge of existence with no way to retreat.

She couldn't speak the words she needed to say, except to utter them inside her mind.

The form moved closer, its hands reaching for her through the mist.

The fingers were covered in blood, the nails black with it.

Anna's mind started to scream as the fingers wrapped around her throat, icy bands of death she couldn't escape.

Her breath stuttered beneath the pressure of those steely fingers. Her body twitched without moving. Death beckoned and Anna knew she'd drift away into the ether when she was gone, never even returning to the life she could still feel hovering behind her, or the man waiting for her to return.

Tears froze on her cheeks. Desperation made her mind howl with regrets as the fingers tightened further, the impossible pressure crushing her throat.

Someone called to her. It was a familiar voice she couldn't quite place. The memory was frozen in the mass of unreachable thoughts in her mind.

The voice became desperate, screaming her name into the mist, where it was swallowed up and pulled away as if it had never existed.

Then the mist shifted.

It rolled violently past the form with the hate-filled gaze.

The pressure on her throat eased, then returned, and Anna felt her life ebbing away.

Thunder. An enraged howl. And the murderous presence was ripped away from her in a whirlwind of fear and fury.

Anna felt the first, tentative touch of life. Pinpoints of warmth spread across her back. She tried to reach for it, her mind screaming a name only her heart recognized. But the warmth didn't come any nearer.

She had no feet, no mind, no ability to move in that direction.

The mist shifted again, sending waves of brittle fog to pummel her immobile form.

Thunder rolled through the fog. Anger rode the thunder, touching her skin like prickles of electricity.

Suddenly another presence was there, directly in front of her. Intense dark blue eyes peered at her through the mist and for the briefest second, a handsome face flashed clear. An angry voice pierced the mist like a blade. *What are you doing? You don't belong here!*

She imagined lifting a hand to that face, feeling love that had no genesis as her fingers touched a bristly chin, slipped over skin she'd never touched before.

Joss…

Her heart swelled beneath the affection in that dark gaze.

He shook his head, perfect lips tightening on a grimace. *You've lost your dang mind, darlin'.* And before she could respond, he reached up and grabbed her shoulders, giving her a hearty shove that propelled her out of the blustery mist, and into a warm pair of arms in a softly lit room.

CHAPTER EIGHTEEN

Anna sipped the hot tea Pratt had begged from Milo and tried to stop shivering. She gritted her teeth against another round of teeth clacking just to try and wipe the worried expression off Pratt's face.

"I can't believe that thing pulled you back in." He shook his head. "No more ghosty stuff for you until I talk to Morty. Maybe she'll have an idea how to rid you of that thing."

Anna grinned. "Ghosty stuff?" She sighed. "At least I know Joss is all right."

Pratt fixed her with a look. "Oh man. You're going to get such a lecture…"

She shuddered and it wasn't from the cold. "I might need to stay away from the store for a few days. Maybe a month. He looked really mad."

Pratt chuckled. "Take your medicine, Miss Anna."

"Hey!" she objected. "It was as much your idea as mine to try to bring Rebecca here."

He tried to look innocent. "Me? I have no idea what you're talking about."

She grinned around the mug. A door in the outside room closed and voices rose. Anna flashed Pratt a look. "We need to get out of here."

"You need a few more minutes. The Millers will just have to deal with it."

A shadow fell over the rug and Pratt and Anna looked up to find Greg Miller glaring at them. "What are you two doing here?"

Anna squared her shoulders. "Probably the same thing you're doing."

Miller strode into the room, his handsome face set in a scowl. Young Martha slouched in behind him. She was clearly not excited about being there.

The teen gave them a petulant look and wandered over to the seating area at the side of the room, pulling out her phone and tapping on it with both thumbs.

Greg poked a finger at Pratt. "You have no right…"

Pratt raised a hand, stopping him mid-sentence. "We have as much right as you do to be here so just zip it. I know you think you own everything and everyone but you are mistaken. I'm happy to be the first one to break it to you."

Miller's face turned red but he made a visible effort to calm himself. Finally, he inclined his chin. "You're right. I can't dictate who should be here and who shouldn't. I've already fought this battle and lost." He shook his head, looking disgusted.

Anna set her mug on the table and sat forward. "Fought what battle?"

Miller glanced toward the door and then back down at her. "Maybe if you stuck your two cents in, Milo would see reason." He sat down on the other end of the couch.

Anna barely restrained herself from scooting farther away.

"Milo is allowing that pederast, Pastor Fredrick to officiate the funeral. Maybe if you objected too…"

Anna held up a hand. "Hold on. You're calling Pastor Fredrick a child molester?"

"Of course. Surely you know his history with the Dasherys?"

"I know he used to council Celeste," she said, anger rising and warming her like a gallon of tea couldn't have. "Do you have proof he was ever inappropriate with her?"

"You two have been snooping around enough to have heard the rumors that they were lovers."

Pratt shook his head. "Rumors aren't facts, Miller. Besides, we've been told that Celeste Dashery already had a boyfriend."

Miller snorted dismissively. "Easterman? He wasn't interested in Cele. He was panting after Willa from the time they were toddlers in the sandbox."

Anna felt her eyes go wide. "Your sister and Henry Easterman were...?"

"Of course not! You two are pretty pathetic investigators if you haven't ferreted out yet that my sister is a lesbian."

"Greg!"

They all turned to find Willa standing in the doorway, her pretty face flushed with anger.

Miller didn't even look chastised. He waved his hand in brisk dismissal. "I'm pretty sure everybody knows, Will."

The woman strode over, her movements choppy with anger. She stopped in front of him and leaned closer, stabbing him in the shoulder with a rigid finger. "Shut up about my business. You have enough trouble dealing with your own life. Stay the hell out of mine."

Miller stood, his face reddening again. "My life is fine. Yours, however, is a hot mess. Just like you are, dear sis."

"Mr. Miller?"

Everyone turned to find Milo Watson standing just inside the door. His small, brown eyes were round with alarm and his pudgy cheeks jiggled. "I need to speak to you in my office please. There's an issue with the...erm...finances."

Greg Miller gave his sister one last glare and left, following Milo into his office.

At that moment, Anna realized she'd given not a moment's thought to how Rebecca Dashery's funeral was going to be financed. "Your family is paying for the funeral?" She asked Willa.

The other woman seemed to shake off her pique, turning her back on the door as if in an attempt to shut out her brother's acidic influence. "There were provisions in her estate and very precise instructions. Greg's handling it because he was her executor."

"Oh." Anna nodded. She slanted a look at the other woman. "I'm surprised he didn't prepare her will."

Willa shook her head. "The old woman had that done by a firm in Indianapolis. Probably because they didn't know her well enough to know she wasn't of sound mind. Not that they would have necessarily cared. Money's money, after all."

Anna nodded. "How are you? You look pale."

Willa rubbed her temple as if fighting a headache. "My brother makes me crazy." Her gaze slid to the casket. "And I'm here to say goodbye to a woman who was a tyrant to me when she was alive. Other than that, I'm just peachy."

"I'm surprised you came," Pratt offered.

She sighed. "I'm doing it for my mother. Mom feels a residual loyalty. After all, the Dasherys did employ her most of her life."

"I can see why she'd feel that way," Anna said.

"Is your mother coming?" Pratt asked.

"The Pastor's bringing her. He's got the church van with a ramp for her scooter."

He nodded. "Your brother just told us he has an objection with the pastor Milo selected for the service tomorrow."

Willa Miller expelled a soft sigh. "Pastor Fredrick." She nodded. "There were some rumors about him being inappropriate with Celeste. People said he took advantage of her because she was simple." Willa frowned. "Celeste wasn't stupid. She was as smart as you or me. Maybe smarter. She was just different."

Anna said. "She would have been what...early twenties when she was spending time with the pastor? Plenty old enough to make her own decisions about romance."

Willa shrugged. "I never believed the rumors myself. But Henry told me once..."

"Easterman?" Pratt asked.

"Yes. He apparently saw the pastor holding Celeste's hands in the gazebo." She shook her head. "I was just glad someone was being nice to her."

"But wasn't Henry Easterman her boyfriend?" Anna asked.

Willa frowned. "To tell you the truth, I don't know what they were. Will you excuse me, please?"

Anna watched her move over to the casket and stare down at Rebecca Dashery with her arms straight down at her sides, hands clenched. Her stiff movements and slumped shoulders were clear signs of the pain Willa Miller didn't seem to want to admit to.

Anna looked at Willa and then toward young Martha, and listened to the raised voices coming from Milo's office. Suddenly she couldn't stand to be there anymore.

She stood up. "Let's go, Pratt."

He glanced around, his handsome face filled with recognition of what she'd seen there. "You sure?"

She nodded. "This isn't where I should be right now. I want to go home."

He dropped an arm around her shoulders and they started out of the room. "You should go to the store and take your licks."

She blanched. "I would but I'm feeling really tired."

He laughed. "You might as well get it over with. Besides, with my luck he'll find a way to haunt me trying to get to you."

She sighed. "Okay. But you'll have my back, right?"

"Are you out of your mind?"

His words were so like what Joss had yelled before he'd shoved her out of the land of the dead and back to the warm embrace of life that it made her smile. Despite Joss' certain anger and Pratt's teasing, Anna knew she had not one but two men who cared enough to fight for her. Being around the unhappiness of the family they were leaving behind made her realize just how lucky she was.

In fact, Anna realized, despite the current mess she found herself in, she might be one of the luckiest people alive.

~SC~

The front door was propped open and the store was like an icebox when they entered. Pratt's gaze slid to Bowler, who was wearing a coat and standing behind the counter, reading the paper. He looked up, his wide, craggy face filled with concern. His nose and the tips of his ears were red, as if he'd spent a few hours in the snow. "Nothing's exploded or crashed in here. No blinking lights. Just the interminable cold." He jerked his head toward the entrance. "I had to open the door to get some warmth."

Anna sighed. "That's a message for me, I'm afraid." She turned to Pratt. "I'd better talk to him alone."

Pratt didn't like it but, for all their differences, he knew Joss would never hurt her. "Leave the door open in case you need to call for help."

She arched a slender brow. "Joss won't hurt me."

"I know. But he's not the only one who likes to crash…sometimes literally…the store."

"Got it." She placed a hand over his, giving it a squeeze. "I'll be fine. You can go home if you want to. It's been a long day."

He shook his head. "Not a chance."

Sighing, she nodded and headed to the back room, her shoulders slightly stooped and her steps heavy. She looked weary beyond the hour. It wasn't really all that late after all, Pratt realized, glancing at the clock. But their journey through Celeste Dashery's life had been an emotionally charged one and Anna was a kind and sensitive soul, her emotions easily enflamed.

At that moment, Pratt felt bad for urging her to deal with Joss before she'd rested. But he knew her well enough to know that she wouldn't rest until she'd made things right between them.

"Rough day?" Bowler asked.

Pratt blinked back to the present as the ex-cop's voice sounded from behind. He glanced around and nodded, scrubbing a hand over his face. "This murder just seems to be getting more complex by the moment." He told his friend about the bodies in the garden at Dashery Cottage.

"No wonder the place is filled with hostile spirits."

Pratt frowned. "And speaking of that..." He lowered himself onto the arm of an upholstered divan Anna had set out front to be recovered after Celeste Dashery had blown through the store. "That thing that grabbed hold of Anna the first day we were in the house..."

Bowler nodded, his gaze filled with interest.

"It somehow grabbed hold of her at the funeral home, when we were trying to contact Rebecca Dashery."

Bowler's face grayed. "Damn."

"Yeah. I don't even want to speculate what that means. I need to talk to the cowboy about it." His gaze slid to the door dividing the front of the store from the back room. Anna had left it open as promised and it was quiet. Too quiet. "But not until he and Anna smooth out their differences."

"From what Morticia and I have figured out, that shouldn't be possible. Ghosts need their anchoring objects to appear. What was Anna touching when she first encountered this spirit?"

"Some homemade cards. But those are in a desk at Dashery Cottage."

Bowler's gaze shifted downward, away from Pratt. "What?" Pratt asked. He didn't like the look on the big man's face.

"I don't know. We should ask Morticia."

"I plan to ask her, but I want your opinion too."

Bowler sighed. "It's possible she's been possessed. If that's the case, Anna becomes the anchoring object and the savage spirit can go wherever she goes."

Pratt's stomach turned to ice and he was glad he was sitting down. "Crap. I really didn't need to hear that." He tried to breathe past the panic. "How do we get that thing out of her?"

"Let's not think the worst. I could be wrong. There could be a less horrifying explanation. Call Morticia and talk to her. It will make you feel better."

Pratt nodded. He glanced toward the open door. "Maybe Joss'll have an idea." *Why was it so quiet back there?*

Bowler's shaggy brows lifted. "What happened between them?"

"Long story. But I think Anna let herself be drawn into the ether and that thing…whatever it was…tried to kill her." Pratt suppressed a shudder. He'd lost a few years of his life watching her choke and gasp as the thing wrapped icy fingers around her throat. He'd nearly died when he realized the danger was beyond the physical plane. In a place he couldn't reach.

"That must have been terrifying," Bowler growled out.

"Yeah. And then some. I can't believe she took that risk."

"You had words about it?"

"No. I wanted to shake her until her teeth rattled. But I figured one of us yelling at her was enough." Pratt let a smile spread slowly across his face. "And this way the cowboy comes out as the villain and I'm the one who *didn't* yell at her."

Bowler laughed, loud and long, at that. "Don't tell me you're competing with a ghost for the lady's attentions?"

Pratt wasn't ashamed to admit it. "If you'd seen how they look at each other you wouldn't be laughing. Besides, they've been together a really long time. I'm a relative newcomer in Anna's life. And the cowboy doesn't waste a chance to remind me of that."

Bowler clapped him on the back, chuckling. "I think you'll be fine, son. I've seen how she looks at *you*. Trust me, the ghost can't give her what she wants."

Pratt shook his head. He wished he could be as sure as his friend about that.

CHAPTER NINETEEN

Anna shivered, rubbing her arms and watching her breath misting out from between her lips as she softly called his name. For the longest moment, she thought he was going to ignore her. But then she shivered violently enough to clank her teeth together and her sweater floated toward her from the hat tree beside the door of her office, settling over her shoulders.

She gratefully pulled it on. "Thanks, Joss."

He eased into view a beat later, his tall form perched on the edge of her desk, long legs stretched out before him.

The cowboy's face was fixed in a glower; his hat pushed back on his head. He was so substantial she could almost see the individual hairs on his bristle-covered jaw. She'd found the chandelier above her head at a salvage store and had known she had to have it. It had been a frivolous gift she'd given herself. Costing too much for a small, dark office room. But it made the space so much brighter and, in that moment, with the light turning his dark blond hair into spun gold that shone under its gilded influence, Anna knew the purchase had been worth every penny it cost her.

"Hey," she said softly.

He continued to look at her, mute and hostile.

Anna offered him a guilty smile. "I know you're ticked at me…"

Ice formed on the floor beneath Anna's feet, covering her desk chair and the desk itself. She looked up as prisms of light painted the walls and saw a truly incredible display of icicles hanging from the chandelier.

She grimaced. "Okay, maybe *ticked* doesn't quite cover it…"

"I'm a site more than ticked at you, darlin'. A far site more." He straightened away from the desk, his big form quivering against the light before reappearing mere inches away. He bent nearer, his face coming close enough to frost her skin.

She pulled her sweater more tightly around her. "In my defense, I never really intended to enter the ether. I just wanted Rebecca Dashery to hear me."

A massive icicle crashed to the floor behind him. "You endangered yourself so you could call that savage spirit back? That woman painted you with blood the last time she showed up." He spun away, his jaw tight. One big hand shoved at the cowboy hat and then grabbed it off his head, flinging it across the room.

The impact from the ghostly object sent more ice skittering downward, the sound like tiny bells as it hit the floor.

"Well, when you put it like that…"

He spun on her, closing the distance between them in a single breath-stealing sway of light. "Darlin' if I wasn't already dead, seein' you in the ether, at the hands of that varmint, woulda dropped me deader than a dormouse in a beat of my non-existent heart." He turned away, flashing to the far side of the small room.

"I know. I'm so sorr…"

He turned back. "I'm in a right pucker, darlin'. I'm so wrathy I don't know if I'm backin' or fillin'."

"I realize that, Joss…"

He blipped back and Anna's nose went instantly numb from the blustery air around him. "I thought I'd lost ya, darlin'. I swan I did."

With those words, some of the starch left him and he seemed to deflate. He eased away from her, putting enough space between them to warm the air in her vicinity. "I'm gonna pound the Puke into last week for lettin' ya endanger yourself."

Anna put up a hand, shaking her head. "Don't blame Pratt. He didn't know what I was going to do. It was all my idea. I scared the stuffing out of him too."

Joss crossed his arms over his chest and settled his butt onto the sill of the room's only window. "Well, that does make up for some of my pain."

She gave him a twisted grin. "I'm so sorry, Joss. I never wanted to scare you."

He grunted, not fully appeased but maybe on his way to it.

"Did you…" She took a breath, unsure how to ask what she needed to know without sending him more deeply into his fit. Finally, she sighed. "I don't suppose you saw who it was?"

"No. The wretched critter kept himself cloaked in ether. But I reckon I'm gonna find out who it is real quick. It's right clear you're in danger. That thing knows you and has no qualms puttin' his hands on ya."

Anna longed to take the fear from his eyes and the anger from his rigid form. "If it makes you feel better, I want you to come home with me tonight."

He lifted his brows. "You don't say."

"I do say, actually." She grinned. "I'm taking the ledger home to look at it again and I'd like you there in case Rebecca Dashery shows up uninvited and tries to paint me with blood again."

He frowned but nodded. "That's one wrathy ghost, darlin'."

Anna couldn't agree more. "It seems like all the spirits in that family are wrathy, Joss."

"Yes, ma'am it certainly does."

Anna unlocked her safe and pulled out the holster that kept Joss tied to the store. She started to place it on her desk, which, thankfully, had lost its sheen of ice, but was wet from the melting. Grabbing a roll of paper towels from the bottom drawer, Anna dried the desk and then grabbed the journal from the safe.

She smiled up at Joss. "Ready?"

He nodded. "Near as can be. I just have ta stop long enough ta pound on the Puke some."

She lifted a brow. "I told you he wasn't to blame."

He snorted out a laugh. "That don't matter none. I was just gonna do it for the pure pleasure of it."

~SC~

Anna dropped onto her bed and sighed wearily. She glanced at the herbal tea on her nightstand, wondering if she should exchange it for something with a little more kick. She was exhausted and wasn't sure she had the energy to pick carefully through the entire journal looking for the words that would make everything clear.

If those words even existed.

Still, she couldn't ignore the fact that the journal had dragged both Celeste and her mother back from the ether. It seemed highly unlikely that a bunch of girlish scribbles would have had the power to accomplish that.

Anna rubbed her fingers over the surface of the journal, noting the slight staining left behind by Rebecca Dashery's gory and wholly undecipherable message. No, the secret to everything had to be there. It had to be somewhere between the pages of Celeste Dashery's journal.

She settled back against the pillows, tugging her robe closer as a chill sprang up in the room. She looked up and smiled at Joss. "Hey."

"Hey, darlin'." His tone was soft, gentle, and filled with all the affection they'd shared over the years. "I just wanted to clap eyes on ya again. Ta make sure you're not feeling all-overish about things."

"I'm fine, Joss. Having you here is very comforting."

He ducked his chin, his wide lips curving with pleasure. "I'll keep out of your way. But if that wrathy varmint comes back I'll know it and I'll be right here."

Anna gave him a smile. "Thanks, Joss."

"No need ta thank me, darlin'. I wouldn't wanna be anywhere else."

He flashed away and the room turned warmer. With a sigh, Anna grabbed the journal and opened its worn and dented cover. She read the childish scrawl in the first section, realizing it was unlikely what she was looking for would be in the early entries.

Anna skimmed through the first twenty pages or so, glad Celeste hadn't been a frequent journaler or she'd have had more than one thick book to wade through.

She couldn't help going back to the idea that there might be other diaries. With everything going on she hadn't had a chance to look for other books in the house. It seemed likely Celeste would have had more than just the one book, thick as it was.

Then she remembered the savage screams of Celeste Dashery's ghost, demanding that she return the book Anna was holding in her hands at that moment.

No. Whatever Celeste and Rebecca thought was important, it was likely in the book Anna was holding.

With that thought, she turned back to the pages, skimming through the typical stories of two girls trying to figure out the world together and navigate their differences in search of friendship. She forced herself to read the expected, fawning descriptions of Greg Miller's supposed perfection.

Anna wrinkled her nose as she read the latter. It was hard to think of Greg Miller as anything but a bully and a snob.

But maybe he hadn't always been so cold and cruel. Celeste described a boy who, at sixteen, handed her a bouquet of flowers he'd picked from the garden and, when Celeste had balked at a ladybug clinging to one of the bouquet's dewy petals, had told her a whimsical story about ladybugs really being fairies in disguise. He'd informed her that she could make a wish and the fairy would grant it.

Though the behavior Celeste described seemed impossible for Anna to imagine, if she looked between the lines of the girl's obvious infatuation and the very genuine feeling the retelling portrayed, Anna came away from the reading with a sense that, if not the knight in shining armor Celeste portrayed him to be, Greg hadn't apparently been nearly the monster his sister described him either.

The truth had to be somewhere in the middle

She briefly wondered what had happened in his life to turn Greg Miller so sour. Then she pushed the question away. His personality wasn't important except for how it fit into the story Anna was trying to uncover.

She read quickly through accounts of Celeste and Willa playing in the garden, pretending they were beautiful brides marrying handsome, wealthy men. She smiled at Celeste's pique over her friend's lack of enthusiasm for the game, and her insistence upon playing the groom to Celeste's bride.

Shaking her head, Anna thought that Willa's early behavior must have been based on confusion about her own sexuality. She could only imagine how confusing that would have been to Celeste.

As Anna continued reading, twenty-two-year-old Celeste described a relationship with her friend, Willy, because she'd begun to call her that to annoy and tease, that seemed to have grown into something much more than friendship. At least on Willa's side.

Anna didn't think Celeste realized how close she and Willa had become. She seemed almost dismissive of her friend's need to spend time with her, and focused her entries more on the time she spent in the company of the men in her life.

She spoke of her walks along the river behind the house with Pastor Fredrick. Painting the events with the color of intimacy. Celeste and the young pastor apparently enjoyed discussing their favorite books, having a shared interest in a popular mystery writer, whose work had a sensual flavor from what Anna had seen. Celeste spoke of Pastor Fredrick grasping her hand with enthusiasm over their discussions and of the warm feelings engendered by that touch.

She talked about Henry Easterman, expressing dismay that he was so often "around". Though her mother apparently encouraged the relationship, Celeste had no interest in his attention and covered page after page of tightly written prose lamenting the fact that he was forever around.

Celeste's entries later showed a softening towards young Easterman, sounding fonder, despite the fact that she often left him in Willa's unhappy company to pursue her literary encounters with the good pastor.

She spent a paragraph worrying that her friend was getting fat and wondering if she too was getting just a little thick around the middle. She swore off pastries with the statement that men didn't like fat women.

That sounded like something Rebecca Dashery probably told her.

As she read on, Anna started to get an uncomfortable feeling about Celeste Dashery's attachment to Pastor Fredrick. She resolved that they should visit the pastor again in the morning. He was starting to look like more of a player in the mystery than she'd first assumed.

The first entry of Celeste's twenty-third year was different from the rest. Looking at the strident slashes of letters across the page, Anna realized she was probably closing in on the key entries.

Celeste's first entry began:

My life has changed irretrievably! I realize after today I will never be the same again. Such pain. Such wonder. I have no words. I must speak to Fredrick. He will know what to do...how to advise me. All I'm really sure about is...Willy and I will never be the same again!

Anna sat back, staring at the words on the page. What did it mean? Had Celeste and Willa become lovers? The words would seem to suggest it.

Anna read on:

HE has been pressuring me incessantly all day. I don't want to give in to him, but he's relentless. Maybe he's right. Maybe this is the chance we've been looking for. But I don't know if I'm ready...

Celeste had used the capped spelling of the word "he" several times over the entries from about age eighteen on. She'd thought at first the girl was referring to her father, who she'd addressed only in the vaguest terms, mentioning walks along the river with him in reference to the walks with Pastor Fredrick.

But at this point in Celeste's life, aged twenty-three, Clifford Dashery was dead.

So, who was "HE"?

They could be initials. Anna's eyes went wide as she thought of Henry Easterman. Could she be referring to him?

Anna shivered, tugging her robe close, and reached for her tea. The drink had cooled and provided no needed warmth. She shoved the journal off her lap and climbed out of bed, shivering again as her feet hit the floor and slipped over...

Ice!

Anna's head shot up, her gaze whipping toward the door.

Rebecca Dashery hovered there, her eyes nearly glowing with emotion as a breeze from the ether sent the flowery dress she wore dancing away from her thick body. Anna remembered the dress from the viewing downstairs.

She realized with a start that Rebecca was finally responding to her summons. Maybe that was why she hadn't come roaring in like a freight train, as she had the last time.

Instead, she hovered there, her iron-gray curls dancing on the same wind that fluttered the hem of her dress. Her mouth was set in a grim line. Her hands clasped high on her torso, reminiscent of her corpse in the casket.

Anna opened her mouth to speak, hoping to keep the ghost from turning savage. "Hello…" She stopped, cleared the rust out of her throat and tried again. "Hello, Rebecca. Thank you for coming."

The ghost wavered on the air, growing transparent, and then turned solid again, several feet closer to Anna.

Anna barely fought the urge to step backward. Her gaze whipped to the journal on the bed. "I've been reading Celeste's journal, trying to find out how she died."

Rebecca's eyes turned dark, narrowing with hostility, and one hand rose slowly before her. Her form blipped again and Anna finally did take a step back as the ghost reappeared only three feet away. She lifted her hands, palms out. "I don't want to cause harm, Rebecca. I'm only trying to help."

The ghost opened her mouth and sent a spine-twisting howl into the air. Anna tried to scamper backward as the hand shot in her direction, blood dripping off the rigid, accusing finger pointing toward Anna's chest.

"Joss!"

She needn't have bothered calling.

He was already in the room, standing just beyond the agitated ghost. His lips moved but Anna couldn't hear a single word he said.

Rebecca Dashery heard him though. She whipped around, the breeze that kept her form in constant, nerve-making motion grew until Anna was caught in its violence. Her long, blonde hair whipped around her head, her robe flew open and she had to grab onto it to keep it on her body.

Joss' lips continued to move. Rebecca's form twitched, growing in turns more transparent and more solid. Anna skimmed around the ghost, keeping as far away as possible, and moved toward Joss while he had Rebecca's attention.

She stepped past her friend, watching Rebecca Dashery's lips move, her words whipped away in the thunderous wind that tore at the bedding and ripped the shades half off her windows.

Debris flew around the room…yellowed pages scrawled with a tight script. Anna panicked, realizing it was the journal.

Rebecca Dashery had shredded it with her rage.

Anna took one step toward the bed and jerked to a stop as Rebecca's hate-filled gaze shot in her direction.

Her lips opened, formed a word, and Anna didn't need to hear the word to know what it was. The ghost shouted, "No!" and then swung an arm, sending something shooting toward Anna like a large, rectangular bullet.

The journal would have smashed into Anna's head, probably knocking her off her feet and giving her, at the very least, a concussion. But Joss flew sideways and the book hit him instead.

"No!" Anna screamed, echoing the ghost, as the sound of ripping filled the air, and bits of yellow paper flew into the air around her like confetti.

In desperation, she reached for the largest chunk of paper she could grab and pulled it close as the violent wind dropped away and the room fell into silence.

The last sound Anna heard was the soft thump of the journal's cover, landing on the rug at her feet.

CHAPTER TWENTY

"Darlin', are you okay?"

Anna looked up into Joss' worried face and nodded. "But the journal is pretty much toast." She fell to her knees on the debris-strewn carpet and started pulling pieces of it together into a pile. She had no idea what she was going to do with the pieces. It would take weeks of painstaking work to tape it all back together again. But she didn't know what else to do.

She couldn't shake the feeling that the journal held information which would help them solve the mystery.

"I'm sorry," Joss told her as he hovered over the mess. "I didn't want it ta clock ya on the noggin."

She smiled. "No worries. I appreciate the goal. It's just that…" Her voice trailed off as she spotted the cover, half underneath the bed. The glossy drops of blood were back, dripped over the exact same spot on the back. "She did it again," Anna murmured.

Joss wavered and reappeared beside the damaged cardboard and cloth binding. "I reckon I don't need ta tell ya that makes me a mite all-overish," he growled out. "No normal ghost should be able ta do what that wrathy spirit did here. And she's done it twice."

Anna nodded. She reached for the cover, pulling it closer and looking down on it. It was open, the inside flat on the floor with only the torn remnants of a few pages left inside. She stared at the childish pictures that had been pasted on the surface of the gingham cloth covering the cardboard jacket. They reminded her of the handmade cards that had started them down the path of trying to solve the murder.

The pictures were glossy and thin like magazine pages and depicted happy families, doing things that happy families did. Sitting around a dinner table together, everyone smiling, watching television, taking walks through areas rich with grass and trees. But Anna touched them with the tip of her finger and she realized they were heavier than magazine paper.

She peeled one away with a fingertip, noting the flattened globs of glue that had held it on the cloth. "Celeste must have decorated this herself." She frowned. "It's a paper and cloth representation of the perfect family unit."

Joss hovered silently, the air around him cool but not icy with strong emotion. Anna figured he wouldn't understand a young girl's longing for love and inclusion. Even if he shared a similar upbringing to Celeste's, men just weren't all that emotional. They tended to view things in more practical ways.

She stared at the thing for a full minute before she realized what she was seeing. There was a thickness beneath the cloth that the pictures had been hiding.

"There's something here," she said, her voice rising with excitement. Anna carefully peeled the cloth away from the inside of the cover and pulled it away from the cardboard. A yellowed square of paper fluttered free, landing on her lap. She picked it up and unfolded the sheet. "It's a letter," she told Joss, flashing him a look.

He eased backward and settled himself onto the edge of the bed. "What does it say?"

Anna began to read:

Today I became afraid.

HE's become so insistent lately, urging me to give in. I don't like the way he's looking at the baby. It's such a tiny thing. So helpless and needy. And I can't seem to make it stop crying even for a moment. Mother will hear if I don't keep him still. And she'll take him away from me. From us.

I can't let that happen.

HE won't stop talking about being a family. It's what I want more than anything. But I don't want it this way. Do I?

I've dreamed of it for so long. But now that the baby's here…I don't know if I can do it.

If only he'd stop squalling, maybe I could think.

Mother's going to hear. She's going to take him away. HE's trying so hard to convince me.

But I just can't think. And I'm afraid HE's going to do something terrible if I don't do what he's asking.

Anna frowned down at the page. She ran a fingertip over the uneven edge, where it had clearly been torn from the journal. Celeste had written it into her diary and then changed her mind, probably deciding it was too dangerous to leave in plain sight.

"What in tarnation did all that mean?" Joss asked, glowering down at the letter in Anna's hand.

She chewed the inside of her lip, feeling as if they were getting close to the truth. But they were still missing a really big chunk of information. "It means we need to talk to Willa Miller again."

~SC~

Pratt listened to Morticia talk, her words coming through the phone with as much urgency as she could project. His pulse pounded with the information. Dread flooded his system with adrenaline.

When Morty stopped talking there was a long beat of silence between them. She filled it with a question. "Pratt, do you understand what I'm telling you?"

He hesitated a fraction of a second longer and then sighed. "Yes. But I don't like it."

"There's no other way. Anna has been possessed by this spirit. If it didn't happen the first time, at the house, she surely didn't escape it the second time at the funeral home. It takes only a small fraction of the spirit's energy to let him in. A tiny spark of electricity embedded in her brain to give him access to her. She'll never be free of that ghost until she returns to the house and faces him again."

"That sounds dangerous."

"It is. Extremely dangerous. She'll need all of you around to help her. Her guardian spirit, you, Bowler. And anyone else you can employ to help anchor her to the world. She's going to have to touch the ether again and repel the spirit. It's the only way."

Silence beat against his ears as he chewed on her words.

"Pratt?"

"I'm here. I'll talk to her about it. But dangit, Morty. I'm not calling you for advice again. Your advice sucks."

"Sorry, buddy."

"Yeah. So am I."

"Let me know what happens?"

"Yeah. I'll talk to you soon."

~SC~

Anna glanced over at Pratt as they pulled up in front of Willa Miller's condo. He'd been so quiet during the drive. His handsome face was lined with tension, his jaw taut. "Are you sure you don't want to talk about it?"

He glanced her way as he put the truck into *Park*. "I do want to talk about it. I *need* to talk to you about it, actually, but not now. Let's get this mess behind us first."

She put her hand on the door handle. "You sure? I'm a good listener."

To her surprise, his frown deepened. "I know."

Willa Miller didn't answer her door when they knocked. Pratt pointed to the white Lincoln MKX parked in front of the condo. "That's her car. I'm pretty sure."

Anna glanced toward the muddy ribbon of the river in the near distance. "Maybe she's out back?"

"It's worth a try. If she's on the balcony we can yell up to her until she gives in and answers the door."

Anna grinned. "That should entertain her neighbors."

He shrugged, his face still serious. She was really starting to worry. Pratt was rarely so tense and when he was, it was with good reason.

A reason that usually had to do with ghosts. A light bulb flared in her mind as they walked around the end of the building. "You know, I was perfectly safe last night. Joss had it well in hand."

Pratt blinked, turning to her. "What? Oh, yeah, I know that. But I'm not thrilled you didn't let me know what you had in mind."

"So, you could come to stare at me while I read?" She shook her head, looping her arm through his and resting her head briefly on his arm. "It wasn't necessary. And Joss is better equipped to deal with problems of the spiritual kind."

His jaw grew so tight she could almost hear the bones grinding together. She stared at him for a moment, wondering what she could do to get him to talk.

"There she is," Pratt said softly as they reached the back. Anna shaded her gaze with her hand and followed his line of sight. A tall, slender figure stood at the edge of the river, broad shoulders slightly stooped as she stared out at the muddy water.

Willa Miller surely heard them approaching. They didn't even try to be quiet about it. But she didn't turn or give any indication of their arrival.

They stepped up beside her and looked out over the slowly moving water, seeing the long-legged bird standing in a quiet cove, fishing in the quiet water at the muddy edge. "Blue Heron," she told them in a rusty voice.

Anna looked at the other woman and was surprised to see the redness around her eyes, the puffiness that attested to a pretty good crying jag. "My sister has a pond and she gets them there every year. The dogs always chase them off." Anna smiled, remembering the phone call from her older sister exclaiming with excitement when the bird first arrived on their property. "You don't expect to see them this far north."

Willa nodded, her gaze never moving from the surprisingly graceful bird. "This one stays through winter. I worry about him every year, afraid he'll freeze or starve."

They stood in silence for a moment, until something startled the Heron and he flapped his enormous wings, pounding the air with a seemingly painful effort to lift his big body above the water.

His leaving seemed to snap Willa out of her reverie. She turned and started walking along the asphalt pathway that followed the river's winding progress.

Pratt and Anna fell in beside her. They didn't speak. Willa had surely heard about the discovery in the Dashery Cottage garden by then. They'd let her speak to any knowledge or lack thereof without prompting.

She looked up into the trees as she walked, a graceful stroll with her hands jammed into the pockets of her loose slacks. She still hadn't looked them in the eyes. Finally, she spoke, staring straight ahead. "I knew you'd come. After…"

"After what?" Pratt urged.

She shot a quick look his way, as if to judge his mood, and then set her gaze on the path ahead. "The bodies." She didn't seem surprised.

"You knew they were there?" Anna asked.

"I did." She turned to Anna. "I don't know what happened. He was fighting with Celeste and then…" She sighed. "By the time the old lady and I got there, he was dead."

"Easterman?" Pratt asked.

"Yes."

"What about the baby?" Anna asked gently, her voice filled with aching for the tiny life lost.

Willa's lips quivered, she pulled air into her lungs in a shaky breath. Tears slipped from her eyes. "Nobody knew. Not even Celeste. I was a big girl. Made myself bigger on purpose to hide it."

Anna blinked, shared a surprised look with Pratt. "The baby was yours?" Incredulity filled her voice.

"Yes. Henry wanted to keep it. He wanted to be a family." The tears flowed faster down her cheeks and her chest heaved once on a sob.

Anna was struck by the similarity of Henry Easterman's sentiment to the letter Celeste wrote. Surely there had to be a connection. "What happened?"

She sniffed, shook her head. "Celeste found me in the bathtub. I was trying to have the baby alone, trying to stay quiet so no one would know. But she found me and she was so sweet, so gentle. She helped me birth him and, when he was born, she wrapped him in a towel and sat there, looking down at him with such love shining in her eyes. I was happy for that one moment. My world was complete. I had everything I needed right there, in that small cocoon." Her expression turned bitter. "But it all ended too soon. Mother came home."

"She found you?"

"No. I begged Celeste to keep him quiet…" She turned her gaze to Anna's, tears shining in her pretty gaze. "We named him Clifford, after my father."

Anna nodded, reaching to clasp the other woman's hand. It was like ice. Willa squeezed her hand hard, holding on as if her life depended on it.

"She managed to quiet him. Then she told me she was going to take him to her room and make him a bed. I nodded, because I didn't want my mom to know about him." Her expression turned sad. "She kept him in her room and I visited him there. We made plans." For a moment, true joy lit her gaze. But it didn't last. "Suddenly she wouldn't let me see him. For two days I didn't see my son. Celeste told me my mother was suspicious, had been asking her questions, and advised I stay away."

"What happened to him?" Pratt asked.

"I don't know. A couple of days later I heard Celeste and Henry arguing in the library. I rushed in there, intending to demand that Celeste give me little Cliff back. I'd decided to face my mother, to tell her about the baby and that Henry and I would be getting married. But Henry was…" She wore a look of such perplexity on her pretty face, it was painful to see. "He was gone too. I had nothing again. No one."

"The baby was dead?"

"Celeste finally admitted she'd accidentally smothered him trying to keep him quiet." Anger replaced the confusion in her expression. "She'd buried him. And she gave me some outrageous tale about a ghost killing Henry. I don't think I've ever been madder at anyone in my life. She'd taken everything from me. I accused her of being jealous. We had a terrible fight."

"And you killed her?" Pratt asked gently.

Willa's eyes went wide with shock. "No! I couldn't have killed Celeste. Despite everything, I still loved her. Even though I knew we could never be together, I loved her and couldn't have hurt her."

"But I don't understand," Anna said. "Who *did* kill her."

Willa shook her head. "I don't know. I guess it might have been whoever killed Henry." Her lips twisted in a bitter smile. "Maybe it was the ghost," she said angrily.

Clearly, she didn't believe that, but Anna and Pratt shared a look. If the same ghost had killed Celeste that had killed Henry Easterman, they'd been set a merry chase by one Josiah Baumgartner.

Willa pulled her hand from Anna's and stopped walking, her gaze sliding away from them. "I'd like to be alone now."

"Just one more question," Pratt said. "Did you bury Henry Easterman in the garden?"

She hesitated a moment and then sighed, nodding. "Father Fredrick helped me. He took me to the place where they'd buried the baby." Her expression went hard. "Celeste had begged him to help her and sworn him to secrecy."

"He helped bury both bodies?" Anna couldn't believe the pastor would have been involved in something illegal.

"He had a fondness for Celeste. I don't know if it was unhealthy. There'd been rumors that he'd been run out of another town for being overly fond of a young girl there." She shrugged. "He was young too. I suspect his judgment wasn't the best. The old lady made him stop coming to the house after he helped me with Henry. I think it was her way of keeping things quiet."

Pratt thanked her. "We'll be in touch."

"Will you…" She seemed to be trying to decide how to ask. Finally, she pushed her shoulders back and lifted her chin. "Will I be arrested?"

"I don't know. That's obviously up to the police. But if you didn't kill anyone, we'll do what we can to help you."

She nodded and turned away. They watched her walk along the path for a moment. Anna felt so sad for the other woman. "That was a horrible story," she breathed.

"Yeah, it was," Pratt agreed. "Unfortunately, we still don't know who killed Celeste."

CHAPTER TWENTY-ONE

They didn't need Bill's verification that the body in the grave was Henry Easterman but it was a tidy little check mark in the *Solved* column. Unfortunately, there weren't a lot of those. Pratt quickly filled the cop in on their conversation with Willa Miller and Bill said he'd get DNA from Willa to verify the baby's parentage.

"What are you two up to now?" Bill asked.

"We're about to speak to Pastor Fredrick again."

"Anything I need to know there?" Bill sounded slightly distracted but Pratt knew he was down a couple of officers, with vacation time, and had his hands full. "Not yet. I'll come in and help you write all this up when we get to the bottom of it."

"Thanks, Pratt. I should just go ahead and deputize you two." He said it with a chuckle, but Pratt cringed at the prospect. "The last thing I want is to be a cop again, Dresden. Even one with a toy deputy's badge."

Bill chuckled. "I can try to get you a real one if that will make you happy. I'm getting low on the cereal box badges anyway."

"Ha. I'll talk to you later," Pratt said on a grin. He turned to Anna. "Ready?"

She nodded. "As ready as I'll ever be."

They climbed out of his truck and headed for the familiar home. As before, the front door was open and they found themselves looking through the screen door, up a flight of stairs to the main level.

Pratt knocked and got no response.

If Agnes Miller had been sitting in her usual spot, she'd have seen them coming. She was either not there or…

Pratt knocked a second time, more loudly. Then he opened the screen door a crack and called up to her. "Mrs. Miller. It's Pratt Davies and Anna Yesterday. The secretary at the church told us we could find Pastor Fredrick here."

There was movement above and the pastor appeared, looking down at them. He had a tight smile on his distinguished face. "Hello, Pratt…Anna. What can I do for you?"

"Can we come inside, Pastor? We just had a couple more questions for you."

Fredrick glanced sideways, in the direction of the living room where Agnes Miller no doubt sat in her little traveling wheelchair.

"Come on in, folks," a strident voice called out.

Pratt opened the door and ushered Anna in ahead of him. She climbed the stairs and offered the pastor her hand. "Pastor Fredrick. How are you?"

He clasped her hand in both of his. "I'm just wonderful. How's the investigation going?" Pratt noticed that his eyes didn't quite meet the smile the curving lips represented. Clearly, he was nervous about what they were going to ask.

"I think we're getting really close, Pastor."

He nodded. "I heard you found a couple of bodies on the grounds." He wore a carefully neutral expression but his fingers were twined together so tightly in front of him the knuckles were white.

"We did. In fact, that's what we wanted to ask you about."

His graying brows rose. "Me? Whatever for?"

"Willa Miller told us about the baby. She told us there was an argument between Celeste and Henry Easterman and that Henry ended up dead."

The pastor opened his mouth to speak but Pratt didn't give him a chance.

"She told us," Pratt went on, "that you helped bury him."

Agatha Miller sucked in a surprised breath. "Is that true, Pastor?"

Fredrick's gaze shifted quickly to her and back to Pratt again. He lifted his hands. "Maybe we should do this somewhere else. I don't want to upset Mrs. Miller."

"Don't be silly, Pastor. Is it true?" Agatha Miller asked.

The pastor shook his head and gave them a nervous laugh. "I really think…"

"She also said you helped bury the infant."

Frederick choked, doubling over with both hands on the stair railing as he coughed and sputtered.

"I'll get him some water," Anna said, heading into the kitchen.

Pratt let his gaze slide to Mrs. Miller. She didn't look surprised by the mention of an infant. "Were you aware your daughter'd had a baby, Mrs. Miller?"

Pastor Fredrick took the glass of water from Anna and thanked her, drinking deeply.

To her credit, Agnes Miller pursed her lips, frowning as she nodded. "I never knew she was pregnant. The girl hid it from everyone."

Pratt nodded. "Celeste helped her birth it."

"Yes. Wilhelmina told me Cele had helped." She said nothing more. Her face blank of emotion.

Pastor Fredrick tried again, "I'd really prefer to discuss this somewhere else."

"I'm sorry, Pastor," Pratt said. "This has to do with her too."

"It's old news," he said.

"Not to the dead," Anna said in a strange voice. Her voice sounded husky, like she needed to clear her throat.

Pratt threw her a look.

"The dead can't rest until they get their vengeance," Anna said.

Pratt's blood ran cold. He turned away from Pastor Fredrick, whose gaze had gone wide with horror.

Anna stood a few feet away, her expression murderous and her gaze fierce. She held a kitchen knife in her hand, a really big one, and Pratt realized she must have grabbed it when she went to get the pastor's water. She wasn't looking at Pastor Fredrick. She was staring at Agnes Miller.

"Anna?"

Pratt moved, intending to grab the knife, but she stepped closer to Agatha, lifting the knife. She spared only a quick slashing glance to halt him. "Stay back. This isn't your concern."

"Who are you?" Pratt asked.

Agnes Miller's eyes were round and slightly bulging, her mouth hanging open as she scanned a look from Anna to Pratt. "What's going on here?"

"Don't you recognize me, cop? Josselin Zebediah did try to warn you. You really should have listened."

Baumgartner!

"What are you doing? You need to leave Anna alone, right now."

"Or what?" Anna laughed. "You have no power in the ether."

"No, but you're in the physical plane now. I have considerable power over that."

She laughed again. Watching Anna closely, Pratt flinched when he saw a quick slide of an ethereal face superimposed over hers. Josiah Baumgartner was clearly enraged and his anger was focused on the woman in the wheelchair.

"You can't do anything, cop. Not while I'm nestled safely inside the woman you love."

Rage brought stars sparking before Pratt's gaze. He clenched his fists. The spirit was right. While Josiah squatted inside Anna, there was nothing he could do. He wouldn't harm her to stop the ghost.

Pratt's mind spun, trying to come up with something he could do to stop Baumgartner. He eyed the fireplace poker. Lead repelled spirits, if only temporarily. But it would also hurt Anna. Badly.

That wouldn't do. He'd give anything for Bowler's nifty salt bullet shotgun.

His eyes went wide. He half turned toward Fredrick. "Salt!" he whispered, flicking a hand toward the kitchen. The other man frowned but Pratt swung his hand violently toward the kitchen again and returned his attention to Anna. She'd taken a couple of steps closer to Agatha Miller and the older woman had backed her wheelchair as far as she could.

Her veiny hand shoved the lever in reverse, and the engine whirred desperately as the tiny tires spun uselessly against the carpet. "What do you want with me?"

Josiah's form briefly morphed over Anna's, and he bared his teeth as he glowered down at the woman.

Agatha gave a short, sharp scream and pressed back in the chair.

She'd seen him.

"You are a foul and petty woman," Josiah ground out in Anna's distorted voice. "You couldn't bear to see my girl happy. You tortured her in life and you've destroyed her spirit in death. My only regret in ripping your foul presence from life is that you will infest the ether with your rotting presence."

Pratt's eyes widened. "Agatha killed Celeste?"

Ice formed on every surface of the small living room, coating the carpet and the walls and the furniture in a layer thick enough to need a chisel to break.

The morphed form of Josiah Baumgartner spun on Anna's delicate frame like a wind spinner on a post. He glared at Pratt through rage-glazed eyes. "Celeste loved me. She was going to come into the ether with the child and we would be a family. But that hag couldn't stand the idea of

Celeste being happy. She wrung the life from the child, letting Celeste blame herself for its death, and then, when Celeste's mind finally broke, she wrung the life from her too."

Anna surged forward, the tip of the knife resting against Agatha Miller's creased throat.

"Anna! You need to fight it."

Her slender frame shuddered, the knife lowering as she seemed to fold in on herself for a beat and then straighten, her head coming up.

A cruel smile found her lips and ice that had nothing to do with the savage spirit inhabiting Anna's body danced up Pratt's spine.

The icy carpet crunched as Pastor Fredrick moved up behind Pratt and pressed a circular box of salt into his open hand.

A foul-smelling breeze had sprung up with the ice and it tore at the draperies, lifting the craftwork from the basket beside Agnes Miller's chair, and hurling a flight of glossy magazines into the air like drunken birds.

It sent Anna's long blonde hair snapping around her face and threatened to blow her off her feet.

Pratt needed to do something fast or she was going to have to live the rest of her life with the knowledge that Agatha Miller had died at her hand.

Pratt glanced toward the pastor and found him on his knees, the large cross he wore around his throat clutched in one hand and his eyes closed. He was murmuring something that Pratt figured was a prayer.

He'd take the pastor's prayer. He'd take anything he could get in that moment.

First he had to get Josiah Baumgartner out of his helpless host.

But he needed a diversion. Fortunately, Agnes Miller inadvertently gave him what he needed.

"She was a spoiled brat! Her parents ignored the fact that she was as crazy as the day was long and treated her like a princess all her life. What about my poor Willa? She couldn't help that she was an awkward girl. She wasn't comfortable enough with herself to befriend others. Not like Celeste. Madness apparently gave her confidence."

Anna's hand twisted and Agatha cried out. A ribbon of blood slipped through the deep creases in the woman's throat. "Your daughter wasn't pathetic!" Josiah shrieked in Anna's distorted voice. "*You* were! Willa was a good friend to my Celeste. She loved her. But you couldn't stand that a daughter of yours would love someone you'd painted as crazy." The knife twisted again and more blood oozed from the wound.

Agatha screamed, her hands lifting helplessly off the arms of the chair. "The girl was mad! Wilhelmina could have done so much better for herself. Even in her pitiful state she managed to get a man and a child. Celeste was never going to be a normal woman. She was better off dead, where her very presence wouldn't be a constant reminder to my poor girl of what she'd lost."

The irony was thick. Everything Willa lost was because of her mother.

Agatha narrowed her mean little eyes and focused them on Anna.

Pratt moved slowly up behind Anna as Agatha Miller seemingly lost her mind and all but guaranteed her own demise.

"You killed the man who was going to make my Wilhelmina happy." She stabbed a bony finger at Anna. "You, threw him against that wall. I saw it happen. I knew he was dead by the way his broken body slid to the floor. *You* are the one who broke my sweet girl's heart. And in that moment, I knew you had to suffer as she was."

Anna's frame seemed to swell as Josiah rose above it, rage making him restless. He surged closer to Agatha and wrapped ghostly fingers around Anna's, intending to press the knife deeper.

Agatha's small eyes went wide, her mouth came open and the knife sank ever so slowly another quarter inch into her flesh.

Moving quickly, Pratt grabbed Anna's arm and poured the salt over her head, screaming her name as Baumgartner's ghostly form spun around and rose up into the air, writhing and screeching his rage as the salt made the return to his host an impossible thing.

"Out, demon!" screamed Pastor Fredrick. "I banish you to the depths of Hell where you will stay for the endless time of your foul existence!"

Pratt flung a last handful of salt at the spirit as he made a threatening surge toward Anna.

"Out, demon!" the pastor screamed again.

Pratt realized the pastor had been reciting a prayer of exorcism when he'd been murmuring before. He didn't know if it would work, but he knew what might. "Anna." He pulled her into his arms, surrounding her with love as he whispered urgently into her ear. "You need to shove him out, honey. He can't stay if you don't let him. Push him out, Anna. I'm here. I've got you."

She shuddered violently, the movement starting at her head and twisting the whole of her body down to her feet. And then her eyes fluttered once and popped open. She didn't move, but her lips started to curve upward into an evil smile.

And ice formed on Pratt's spine again.

~SC~

Anna's body jerked upward off the floor like a marionette on strings. She felt it happening, knew when she flung out her hand and Pratt went flying across the room. She screamed in horror, trying to turn her head to see if he was all right. But just as when the knife had been sliding into Agatha Miller's throat, Anna had to watch, screaming helplessly, from inside her high-jacked body.

169

Josiah's ethereal form expanded, spreading to the very edges of her frame, and threatened to spill out of her skin as rage spun into a whirlwind inside him.

He jerked her arm upward, jabbing her finger toward the helpless woman cringing in the chair, one veiny hand covering the wound on her throat. "Yes! I killed that yellow-bellied coward, Easterman. He believed Celeste killed the babe." Anna's lips opened and the most horrible, grating laugh ground out through them.

Pain sliced through her throat from the unaccustomed and brutal use of her body. She tried to focus on the murmuring nearby. Pastor Fredrick. He was doing something that made Josiah angry. And the ghost was yanking her around to face him...

No! Anna fought to keep her arm from flying up. She could feel the energy bubbling within her that Josiah would use to fling the older man across the room. His ugly thoughts were hers and it was becoming increasingly difficult to separate them from her own.

"Out, demon!" Pastor Frederick screamed. His own voice was hoarse, as if he'd been screaming for a while.

Her hand jerked and the man stumbled backward, falling over a body lying across the floor.

Pratt!

Before Josiah turned away, back toward the helpless Agatha, Anna skimmed a horrified gaze over Pratt's unmoving form, silently willing him to get back up so she'd know he was okay.

A door slammed below and Josiah's gaze shot to the stairwell.

A big man was thundering up the stairs. Anna fought to remember who he was.

She should know who he was! Panic swirled through her. She was losing herself to the savage spirit taking her for a ride like a cheap Honda.

She wasn't going to let that happen. Anna gathered herself together and tried to expand...to push the foreign presence away.

She felt Josiah's start of surprise, then heard his chuckle in her mind. "You can't beat me. In this as in cards, I'm unbeatable."

She'd see about that.

The big man was yelling something. She forced her gaze to his, dragging an irritated Josiah with her.

"...into the ether, Anna!"

She frowned in the tiny space that was left of her. Ether? Why would he want her to go there? Joss would kill her... Anna jerked, her hands coming up to blast the man. She fought the movement, expanding, expanding, pushing against the foreign presence.

She thought it was useless but then she gained a tiny fraction of space.

Josiah raged in her mind as he scrambled to regain it.

"...ether!" the big man yelled as he knelt down beside Pratt.

What was he holding?

Realization hit Anna like a train. She stumbled backward, pulling Josiah with her, and then let the room slide away from her awareness, and reached toward the icy fog with its tendrils sunk deep into Josiah Baumgartner's presence.

She could feel the ghost's confusion as she stopped pushing on him and reached instead for the tethers that held him in the spiritual plane.

Like Joss and Bess and other ghostly forms, Josiah could reside temporarily in the physical plane. Especially if he'd managed to gain a foothold in an unfortunate host as he'd apparently done to Anna. But they could never completely escape the ether. It was always there, hovering in their awareness, tugging them back.

Anna had only to envision the tether, narrow her gaze and see the iridescent length of it stretching away into the fog. It was finer than the finest thread but strong enough to hold a spirit for the whole of its long existence.

She grasped it with her mind, slipped mental fingers along its length, and saw ahead the shimmering shadow of the icy mist. Anna tightened her mental grasp over the tether, wrapped her thoughts around it, and yanked.

They slammed back into the ether and Josiah stumbled away from her, bellowing with rage.

The ether barely had time to embrace them before an enraged tempest slammed into Josiah, sending him deep into the miasma.

Anna stood there helplessly, fighting the residual effects of Josiah's claim upon her senses. She tried to remember why she was there and what she'd been trying to do.

With half of her awareness she watched the spinning gusts of energy pounding against each other in the distance, sending the blustery fog into turmoil that spun with shadows and rocked with screams and curses.

The mist prickled against her skin, aching and then numbing as she stood there, watching the battle before her and not knowing what to do.

Something niggled.

A warm thread tugged at her mind. A memory...a fear...whispered.

The battle spun closer. She recognized the enraged roar of one of the combatants.

Joss!

He was fighting Josiah. Why? She couldn't remember. Then a picture of Bowler holding an old, scarred gun belt flashed through her benumbed brain.

Of course!

Bowler had brought Joss to tell her to go into the ether. He'd known he'd have a better chance of overwhelming the savage spirit there.

Josiah had burst from her as soon as they'd hit the mist.

She was free of him.

Or was she. She looked down, seeing the microscopic gleam of a slender thread, still inserted into her abdomen.

Anna reached down, clasped the thread, lost it. She tried again several times but it was too fine…too slick.

Finally, she closed her eyes and envisioned it. Saw it swirling into her body, twining around her flesh. She shook her head.

"No!" she said firmly. "You don't belong here, Josiah Baumgartner. This is my body. You belong in the ether. Get out of me, and never come back to me again."

The thread tugged hard, pain sluicing through Anna's middle and doubling her over. It felt like someone had grabbed hold of her insides and was trying to rip them out.

But then the pressure eased and, with a final agonizing jolt, gave way.

"OUT, Demon!" Pastor Fredrick bellowed as Anna crumpled toward the floor. She fell fast and hard. But she never hit the ground.

She fell into a warm pair of waiting arms and was immediately lifted off her feet.

She didn't remember what happened after that. Nor what happened for the long, watchful night ahead.

She only learned later that Pratt, Joss and Bowler had gathered to watch over her. That no one slept. No one left her apartment as she tossed fitfully and restlessly on the bed.

But when she finally opened her eyes as the sun rose the next morning. Only one face looked down on her with a terrified, weary gaze.

She lifted her hand to touch his bristled cheek. "Hey."

Pratt closed his eyes and drew a long, shaky breath. "Hey, yourself."

CHAPTER TWENTY-TWO

Pratt clasped her icy hand in his own, wonderfully warm one, lifting it to his lips. Placing a lingering kiss on the back of her hand, he held it against his cheek for a long moment with his eyes closed.

Tears slipped from Anna's eyes. "I'm sorry I scared you."

He shook his head. "It couldn't be helped. It was what you needed to do."

She nodded, sniffling. Then she grinned. "I can't believe, after all the grief he gave me, that Joss was the one who told me to go into the ether."

Pratt laughed, shaking his head. "He was right. Morticia told me that was the only way to get rid of Josiah. But I'll admit I might not have had the strength to tell you to do it. He did what I'm not sure I could have done."

"Where's one o' them recordin' contraptions when I need it?"

They both turned to the door, where Joss stood with a self-satisfied look on his face. "Hey, darlin'."

Anna grinned back. "Hey, you. Thanks for taking care of Josiah for me."

He shook his head, moving into the room to stand next to her bed. Upon closer inspection, Anna could see the lines of weariness around his sexy eyes and the fading quality of his form that spoke of deep weariness. "I didn't do nothin' but keep him busy while you discovered how ta fling him out."

She nodded, then frowned. "Do I need to worry about him coming back?"

Joss sighed. "I expect so. It might be time you finally listened to me and stayed away from that old house. There's more ghosts than's healthy in that wicked place."

She couldn't agree more.

"And along those lines," Pratt interjected. "Greg Miller called me this morning. He said the family's dropping the suit for ownership of Dashery Cottage. He figures, given what his mother did, they don't deserve to own it even if Rebecca Dashery's letter to Agatha was real."

"Sounds like he's finally listening to Willa." She frowned. "I don't want to go back to that house, Pratt."

"I think we can all three agree on that, honey. I can oversee the removal of things you want for the shop and, if you'd like, we can sell the rest in an estate sale. You could sell the house too. Maybe it can still provide some pleasure to somebody, despite its sad past."

"It is a beautiful old place. Let's hold that thought. I have an idea for what to do with Dashery Cottage." Maybe young Martha, who seemed to be searching for a place to call her own, might want the home if Anna donated it to her. At least she could sell it to buy a less "ghosty" place. Anna glanced up at Pratt. "Did you ever learn who knocked you out in the garden?"

"Not yet. But knowing what we know now, I'd place money on it being Willa. She knew her baby was buried there. I'm sure that tiny skeleton was a big part of the reason she's never really been happy."

"That makes sense." Anna gave Joss a crooked grin. "I appreciate you not saying I told you so about Josiah Baumgartner."

He shrugged one shoulder, looking embarrassed. "I shoulda rid the place o' that varmint in the first place. I knew he wasn't no good."

"That wasn't your responsibility, Joss."

"I know, darlin'. But if I'd known what he'd do to you..." His voice trailed off as anger turned the air around him blustery.

She lifted a hand. "Nobody could have known."

"Good idea having Bowler show up with your gun belt," Pratt told the cowboy.

Joss nodded. "He's a rip-snortin' fella. We been wakin' snakes together while you two been flittin' around botherin' folks."

Anna and Pratt shared a look, then a grin, and, finally, a laugh at Joss' interpretation of their investigation.

"Anyways, I knew if I could get Josiah back into the ether I could separate him from you and you could do what ya needed."

"Smart," Pratt said, only half grudgingly.

Joss gave him a rare smile. "Thanks, Puke. You had your moments too. But that preacher fella near flung me out of there a few times with his fancy prayers."

Anna's eyes went wide. "You felt that?"

"Exorcism rites," Pratt said. "I'd always thought that was a lot of hokum."

"Not from where I stand...or float..." Joss said, winking at Anna. "It was like a bee buzzin' around my ears, tellin' me ta skedaddle. And the impulse was gettin' stronger by the minute. If it wasn't for that, I'da took that varmint on right there in the old lady's house."

Anna nodded. "It seems we had all the right ingredients. If we'd only known what we were doing with them."

"What's gonna happen with the old lady, anyways?" Joss asked, frowning. "I looked into that one's soul and it was black as tar. Old Josiah would ha' been better off possessin' her instead."

Pratt nodded. "She's a pretty cold-blooded person, that's for sure. She killed her own daughter's baby just to paint Celeste Dashery with the crime and then, pretending she was trying to help Celeste marry Fredrick, she killed Celeste instead."

"But why'd she kill her?" Anna asked.

"Jealousy maybe. Or because Celeste seemed about to be happy and that was going to hurt Willa, who'd lost everything." Pratt shrugged. "Who knows really. The woman's clearly cray-cray."

"I guess Celeste wasn't in love with Josiah?"

"Not particularly," Joss said, making Anna snap her gaze around in surprise. "I spoke to her some. Never got a chance ta tell ya, darlin', with everything that's been goin' on. That scoundrel had been pesterin' her somethin' awful to come into the ether and stay. But she wanted the preacher man. Always did. And the governess promised she'd fix the deal. It seems there was rumors he had a young wife somewhere's. But the girl was determined. She told the governess to offer a substantial amount of cash to the wife, encouragin' her to absquatulate and keep her yap shut."

That brought Pratt's eyebrows up. "She tried to buy off Fredrick's wife?"

"That was the plan. Though the girl don't reckon Old Mrs. Miller done it."

"Did Celeste Dashery tell you who killed her?" Pratt asked in a warning tone.

"O' course not, Puke! You don't reckon I'da told ya that? She could not recall. You was aware we lose some of our memory when we die?"

Pratt frowned. "I didn't know that."

"It's a rare ghost can recall the last minutes of his life." He shook his head. "I reckon that's a good thing in the long term."

"How did Mrs. Miller make Celeste think she'd killed the baby when she hadn't?"

"From what the girl told me, she was an ether walker such as yourself, darlin'. She could go inside, spend time with Josiah and, apparently sometimes her papa. While she was there…"

"She didn't know what was happening in the physical world," Pratt finished, frowning.

"Yep. All the old woman had ta do was tell the girl she'd been holdin' the child, trying ta keep it quiet, and she'd accidentally smothered it."

"Poor Celeste."

Joss nodded. "But don't waste none o' your sad feelin's on that girl, darlin'. She'll rest easy now it's all been sorted out."

"Which, I believe was Josiah's wish," Anna said softly. Despite the ghost's abuse of her as a host, she understood his motives better than anyone, having shared his mind for a time. "He truly did love Celeste. He only wanted her to be happy. And having the murders unsolved and the murderer unpunished was keeping her from resting."

"As long as he got hisself some happiness along the way," Joss replied with a frown. "He was a hoister, but it 'ppears he wasn't lyin' about doing it for a girl after all."

"But why did he torture you so much?" Pratt asked. "He wanted your help finding a murderer, I get that, but he threatened you several times in the ether. What was that all about?"

Anna shook her head. "I think he was angry at Celeste for rejecting him. And, though he couldn't help trying to find her killer so she'd forgive him and come to him in the afterlife, that anger made him savage." She frowned, thinking there was nothing more terrifying than a savage spirit in the physical world, but dealing with one in the ether would scar her for life.

"That's what we get for trying to help a ghost," Pratt murmured angrily.

In an effort to distract them from the hauntings, Anna asked, "What about Celeste's father? Was he murdered?"

Joss frowned. "Accordin' to the girl, it was an accident. Old Mrs. Dashery had some secret abilities all her own. She could lift objects and move them around with her mind. The girl said the old woman accidentally moved the ladder, not realizin' the girl's daddy was on it."

"Yikes!" Anna said. "That's awful."

Joss nodded.

Anna glanced at Pratt. "What about Willa and Pastor Fredrick? Will they be charged as accessories?"

"That still remains to be seen. But if worse comes to worst, I hear Greg Miller's a darn fine lawyer." He grinned.

"I have to admit I don't get the whole thing with Easterman," Anna told the men. "If Willa's gay, why'd she have an affair with Henry in the first place?"

"I reckon I can clarify that one," Joss told her. "That girl was tryin' whatever she could to catch Celeste Dashery's attention."

"You mean she was trying to make Celeste jealous?" Anna's tone was incredulous.

"Reckon so. But when she ended up with child, well, she decided she'd do the best thing for the babe and marry the young man."

"Amazing," Pratt said, shaking his head. "What a mess."

Anna nodded sadly.

"Well, I'm real tired," Joss told them. "I need ta' retire to the ether for a while." Joss slanted a look at Pratt. "If ya don't mind, Puke, I'd like a private word with Miss Anna."

Pratt kissed the back of her hand again and released it, standing. "I'll make coffee. I don't know about you but I'm gonna need it today. Bill wants our help sorting this all out."

She nodded and watched him leave, closing the door softly behind him.

Joss moved slightly, drawing her attention back to him. He stood beside her bed, hat crushed in front of him in his two big hands.

He seemed even more translucent than before. Clearly, he was getting to the end of his reserves. But his entire focus was on her. Whatever he had to say was obviously really important to him.

"What is it, Joss? Is there something wrong in the ether?"

He gave his head a brusque shake and twisted his long-suffering hat in his hands again. "I wanted ta say I was sorry for before." He grimaced. "For yellin' at ya."

Anna sat up, her fingers twitching on the covers with the urge to touch him…to tell him he never needed to apologize for caring about what happened to her. "It's not necessary…"

He lifted a hand to stop her. "Let me get this out, darlin'. It's important."

She sighed, nodding.

"I was wrathy and I took it out on you. That ain't right." He moved incrementally closer, his blue eyes even darker than usual, intense with emotion. "It did scare me that you was there, in the ether. And seein' that varmint's hands wrapped around your delicate throat…well…it just about knocked me into a cocked hat. But that ain't why I yelled."

His image wavered violently and, for a beat, Anna thought she would lose him. She leaned closer, desperate to keep him there. She suddenly knew with all her heart and soul that she needed to hear what he was about to say. "Go on, Joss. Please."

His gaze never wavered from hers. "When I saw you there…when you touched me…" His chest rose and fell on a breath that was pure emotion. "Feeling your fingers on my skin, well, it was as close ta heaven as this old cowboy's likely ta ever get. It shook me, Miss Anna. I reckon I owe ya that truth."

Tears slipped from her eyes. Until that moment she hadn't realized how very much he meant to her. "It was a special memory," she told him. "One I'll never forget."

He nodded. "But that's all it is," he said gruffly. When she tilted her head, feeding all the love she felt into her gaze, he nodded. "No, don't go gettin' all weepy on me darlin'. Save your pity for those that need it. I don't. It's enough for me to share your days and keep you close." He gave her his trademark, crooked grin. "I just wish ya had better taste in menfolk…outside o' me o' course."

She gave him a watery laugh. "You know you like Pratt."

"Like? Not so much, as those in your world would say. But I respect the hell out of him. Because he wants the same thing I do. He'd die tryin' ta keep ya safe, darlin'. And that's all I can ask of any man." He nodded once as if satisfied. "I told ya what I wanted ta tell ya. You'll never hear another word about this from me. Don't expect it. But I thought ya had a right ta know why I was so wrathy."

He started to fade and Anna panicked, moving without thought. She reached out and grabbed his hand and then winced, dropping it as he gave his hand a reflexive jerk.

His eyes went wide. Her eyes did too.

There hadn't been a painful jolt when they'd touched.

She looked at her hand and he looked at his.

"Well ain't that somethin'?"

Anna's gaze lifted to his. "What just *didn't* happen?"

He frowned. "Must be 'cause you was in the ether, maybe?"

"Maybe." She grinned, climbing to her knees on the bed. "Whatever the reason, I'm not going to look a gift horse in the mouth." She gave him a smile. "Come here, cowboy."

His lips curved upward in a slow grin. He extended his arm first, reaching out to touch her tentatively on the arm, his finger lingering there. When sparks didn't happen, he slowly moved closer. Joss stood stiffly as she wrapped her arms around his waist and laid her head on his chest with a sigh.

Then, with exquisite deliberation, Joss wrapped his arms around her too, resting his head on hers.

He closed his eyes.

No sparks. No pain.

Just a drawn-out, contented sigh, filled with enough happiness to last an afterlife.

ABOUT THE AUTHOR

USA Today Bestselling Author Sam Cheever writes mystery and suspense, creating stories that draw you in and keep you eagerly turning pages. Known for writing great characters, snappy dialogue, and unique and exhilarating stories, Sam is the award-winning author of 80+ books.